There Was
an Old Woman

There Was an Old Woman

Elizabeth Davis

PUBLISHED FOR THE CRIME CLUB BY

Doubleday & Company, Inc.

Garden City, New York

1971

All of the characters in this book
are fictitious, and any resemblance
to actual persons, living or dead,
is purely coincidental.

Library of Congress Catalog Card Number 70–131070
Copyright © 1970, 1971 by Lou Ellen Davis
All Rights Reserved
Printed in the United States of America

to Perry Davis

The author gratefully acknowledges the gracious technical assistance of James "The Amazing" Randi.

Chapter One

*

For four days, Amanda Hilton waited in the lobby of the large office building on East 47th Street. She arrived between a quarter and ten of five and remained until the crowds started to thin, about five-thirty. She looked to be in her late fifties, and from her manner and dress might have been a clerical supervisor in virtually any of the companies housed within the building. She was neither slim nor heavy. Her features were pleasant, except for the set of her jaw and lips thinned by years of bitterness. In her gloved hand, she carried a brown leather brief case, approximately the size of a computer printout. It was an odd brief case—scuffed and marred, yet curiously unweathered.

Frank Klaner stepped from the elevator, accompanied by three other members of his department—a programmer, a systems analyst and a project manager. Frank carried a brown leather brief case, scuffed, marred—and weathered.

"Paper tape is *not* going to hold up," said the programmer.

"I know," answered Frank.

"Yeah, but *he* doesn't know," insisted the programmer. "He doesn't know what the hell he's doing—not on this."

"So how are you going to prove he's wrong?" offered the systems analyst. "You're not going to *tell* him. You don't tell that guy anything."

"Hold it," said Frank. "I want to get a paper."

"What time you think we'll be finished?" asked the programmer.

"Midnight," called Frank, over his shoulder, "if we're lucky." He stepped over to the newsstand and bumped into two people on his way. One was a sandy-haired man in his late twenties who seemed oblivious to the crowd, and the second was an elderly woman wearing a nondescript lightweight coat. Frank carried his own coat. It was early June, and the weather was freakish—summer hot then winter cold, sometimes both within the course of twenty-four hours. He placed his brief case on the floor, tucked the newspaper under his arm with the coat, then rooted for a dime. He found one and dropped it onto the counter, then hoisted his brief case and took two steps toward rejoining his associates.

Something was wrong. The brief case. The weight—the feel of it. He stopped and lifted it to where he could take a good look at it. It seemed okay—no, it didn't. It was newer than his, and the weight was definitely not the same.

His vocabulary did credit to his army days. Then, "Hey, Bob—Jim—Pete—hold it."

Their abrupt halt caused a minor traffic jam.

Frank walked to the stairway exit, opened the door, then placed the brief case on the stairs in front of him and opened it. The others glanced at its contents—a stale half sandwich, two unopened reams of manila paper and an apparently new book on flower arranging.

It took a few seconds for the shock to soak in.

Numbly, from Bob, the systems analyst, "Did you have your name in it?"

Two girls, apparently lower-floor employees tired of waiting

for room in an elevator, edged past the group with the brief
case, merging into the now-thinning lobby crowd.

"I'm trying to remember," said Frank. Inside, he was raging.
Approximately eight hundred punch cards, each individually
punched by a crew of girls who had been working all afternoon.
In addition, the information on the cards was confidential.

"Oh, somebody's going to really miss that," offered Pete,
dryly. Pete was the project manager. "That sandwich was part
of a controlled experiment on mold," he continued. His voice
held traces of a southern accent, soft, smooth.

"What do we do?" asked Jim, looking at Frank.

"I don't know." Frank started to sweat. He was a tall man,
dark hair, reasonably nice-looking, thirty-four years old. His
immediate superior was about to leave—recurring bleeding
ulcers, and now—as of the instant Frank's brief case disappeared, Frank was no longer about to step into the job. Could
they really break him for this?

Of course they could. The whole company, from the office
boy on up, was a shark pool.

He glanced at Pete. Pete played all the angles. Pete had
firmly allied himself with Frank so he could ride with him.
Here was where Pete got off. Pete's face was expressionless,
except for his eyes—gray eyes, sharp, wary.

Frank snapped the brief case closed and let out a deep
breath. "Okay, Pete. Call D.S.I. Have them reschedule us for
about eleven—if you can. If not, whatever time they've got.
Then go home if you want to—all of you, but stay available."

"Wait a minute," said Jim. Jim didn't need to play angles.
He was strictly a programmer—a good one, not interested in
the management ladder. "You sure you'll get it back?"

"No," answered Frank, "but it did have my name in it—and
the company name. Seems worth it to go back upstairs and

wait an hour or so. Give whoever has it time to discover the mistake and call."

"And what if nobody calls?" asked Bob.

Frank shrugged his shoulders, but his mouth was dry. "Cancel the machine time. Reschedule for tomorrow." Put all the girls back to work repunching this same data. Other scheduled work for tomorrow would have to wait. Which meant delays bordering on chaos—and the end of any hope for promotion in the foreseeable future. Pete. Pete would probably step in right over him. Could Frank work for Pete, report to Pete, instead of the other way around?

"Anything I can do to help," said Pete, "let me know."

He meant it, too, Frank realized. Pete would help because Pete was smart. Don't antagonize Frank, because Frank still might make it—might get it back.

The programmer took a long look at the brief case. "You know, there's something—strange about that case. Like it fell down a flight of stairs about six times. It's new. Look at the color. The scratches are clean—like all of them were made at the same time. No time for the older ones to get dirty before new ones showed up."

"Yeah," answered Frank, dryly. Anyone who worked with programmers knew they were maniacs for details—any details on anything. Irritably, he hoisted the brief case with his left hand and headed back toward the elevators.

It was a little after five-thirty and the office was virtually deserted. The marketing director was still there, along with one switchboard operator, one junior executive trainee and a secretary.

Frank headed into his office and sat behind the desk, lit a cigarette. It was ironic. If he had his brief case, there were things he could take out of it and use, now, while waiting for it to be returned.

A light flicked off. The marketing director left. Catch the train to Connecticut or Scarsdale or wherever it was. Or did he have a car? One of those large blue Buicks in the company garage. You've got to reach for it—the house, the car. It doesn't just happen. That's what Frank's wife did not understand.

In that instant, he was annoyed because he wanted to call his wife. She wasn't expecting to see him until after midnight. To call now would only be to tell her he might be earlier or later. Nothing was set yet.

He glanced at his watch. Six o'clock. The junior executive trainee left. Was the secretary still there? Probably not.

Call her, for crissake. Call his wife.

No.

At seven-thirty, he slipped into his coat and, through habit, reached for his brief case. This time, however, the brief case was not his. The feel of it was unfamiliar—disconcerting, unnerving. Not really conscious of the thought processes behind his actions, he deposited it on the floor beside his desk and left without it.

The apartment he shared with his wife and two children—a girl, age five and a boy, age three, was on East 80th Street. It was a new building, the rent was ridiculous and the lobby was gaudy.

Frank heard his wife's voice even before he inserted his key in the lock.

"STOP it, Tracy. No, Jimmy, she is not going to change you into a frog. She couldn't, even if she really wanted to."

"I DO want to," came the shrill voice of his daughter, followed by a loud howl from Jimmy.

Frank smiled. Kids were great—in moderate to small doses. He opened the door.

"Daddy, Daddy!" They tore out of the kitchen with sticky hands, dirty faces and hugs.

"Hey, hey, woah—" he said. "Go wash your hands."

Dianne, startled, walked to the kitchen doorway. She wore bluejeans, one of Frank's shirts on which the collar had become frayed and no make-up. At age twenty-eight, she was still an exceptionally attractive woman—slim, well built, shoulder-length ash blond hair and gray-green eyes.

"Oh, for—" said Tracy. Tracy was a beautiful child, even when angry and she was angry now because *she* saw nothing wrong with her hands.

"Come on," said Jimmy. "I'll race you."

"Hey," called Frank, as they rapidly disappeared down the hall toward the bathroom, "no running in the apartment!"

"Nice of you to drop by," offered Dianne, still holding a wet sponge, "and with such a warm welcome for the kids."

The depression that had started when he lost the brief case abruptly dominated every other feeling. "Thanks. It's a real joy to be here."

"Oh, for heaven's sake, Frank. What does it cost to have one suit cleaned? They were excited. Glad to see you. They see you so rarely. What are you doing home anyway? You said you wouldn't be here until after midnight."

"Well, I'm sorry if I interfered with your other plans."

"Stop it, will you? Sit down. Have you eaten?"

The children returned. Ostentatiously ignoring her father, Tracy asked Dianne, "Are you going to read us a story, Mommy?"

"Yes, dear. Get into your pajamas and help Jimmy get into

his." Then, to Frank, "What do you want to eat? We've got beans, canned chili—there may be some frankfurters."

"That's it?"

"Well, I wasn't expecting you," she snapped. "You know I do the week's shopping tomorrow."

"Look, I—I'll go out. Get a steak. I'm sorry. I'm just—hungry." It was true, too, in spite of the upset over his brief case. His lunch had consisted of a cup of coffee and a vending machine package of cheese flavored crackers at D.S.I.—Data Services, Inc., the service bureau that sold computer time to Frank's company.

"So long, kids," he said. "See you later." He knew of course that it was not true. By the time he got back, both of them would be asleep.

His daughter showed no reaction. In that instant, the resemblance to her mother seemed stark. The silent treatment—at age five.

"Bring me bubble gum," said Jimmy.

"We'll see," said Dianne. "Go on. Pajamas."

Abruptly, Frank stared at his wife. She looked young—almost childlike, wearing his shirt. He loved her—always, but in that moment, the intensity of his love dominated every other feeling. He wanted to tell her, but the words stuck in his throat.

"If I get any calls," he said, "I'll probably be back in half an hour—maybe forty-five minutes."

She nodded, and he wanted to tell her it was good to see her. He walked out.

Fifteen minutes later, Dianne was seated on the couch with one child on each side of her, "The Land of Oz," second in the Oz-book series, open on her lap.

The phone rang.

"Oh NO!" announced Tracy, her five-year-old sense of the dramatic well developed.

Dianne left Jimmy proudly in charge of keeping the place marked, then went to the kitchen and lifted the phone receiver. "Hello?"

The voice was female—sounded elderly. "May I speak to Frank Klaner?"

"He's not here right now. Who's calling?"

"Oh dear. Well, I'm afraid there's been a mix-up. It's in reference to his brief case. Seems I walked off with his—he must have walked off with mine, earlier this evening. His had his name in it. I took a chance he lived in Manhattan and looked in the phone book. Is this the right Frank Klaner? Does he work—" She gave the name of the company.

"Yes," answered Dianne. His brief case! Dear Lord, why hadn't he said anything? He must have been terribly upset. Or maybe not. Maybe there wasn't anything particularly important in it. Within the last few years, he'd grown so hard to understand. The aspects of him she'd never really understood seemed to have grown most predominant. "I'm expecting him back in about half an hour," she went on. "May I have your phone number?"

"No, that wouldn't do. My daughter's been quite ill and she's sleeping. The phone would awaken her, so I've kept it off the hook. I'll call him."

"Oh. All right. No—wait a minute—" A key in the lock. "That may be him now. Hold on."

She stepped into the hall.

Frank came in, carrying a small bunch of yellow tea roses. He smiled. "I decided I'd rather have canned chili with you," he said.

Dianne's eyes were suddenly misty. "Nut!" she answered.

Then, "Hey, there's a phone call for you. Something about your brief case."

His body took on the alertness of a prize fighter at Round One. "When?"

"Now. I told them to hold on when I heard your key."

He dropped the roses onto the hall table and hurried into the kitchen.

"Mommy," called Tracy, "are you *ever* going to finish the story?"

"Hello?" said Frank.

"I have your brief case," said the voice, that beautiful, beautiful idiotic female voice. "I was picking it up for my daughter," she continued, "and didn't realize there'd been a mistake until I gave it to her."

"Well, I need it," said Frank. "Badly. Can I pick it up? Where do you live?"

"Six twenty-one West 93rd Street," she answered. "Please do be good enough to bring mine."

He hesitated. Hers was still at the office, damnit. "Okay," he said. "Take me a while to get it. I'll see you around nine o'clock."

Still wearing his coat, Frank stepped into the living room. "I have to go out," he said.

"Where?" asked Dianne. The kids were already in the bathroom.

There was something about her face—her voice. "What's wrong?" he asked.

"I—don't know." Even before the words were out, she decided she was being ridiculous. Of course she felt unhappy—let down. For one brief instant tonight—for the first time in a long time, he had looked at her as though he really saw her. And now—as usual, the computers emerged victorious. What a ridiculous rival! "I'm sorry," she said. "Just tired, I guess. Be sure and eat, will you?"

"Yeah. I'll probably be late. If anybody from the office calls and mentions the brief case, tell them it's okay."

"Yes." She bit her lip to avoid adding the word "sir." Who did he think she was? His secretary? A "please," of course, would have changed the whole complexion of it.

He left.

She put the kids to bed, then—wearily, cleaned the kitchen. She felt—keyed up. It was an odd feeling—one she had not had in a long time, and at first the exact nature of it was difficult to pin point. Frank. Something to do with Frank.

She rinsed the last plate and loaded it into the dishwasher.

The feeling grew stronger. Now she could identify it—sharp and clear. The name of the feeling was fear.

It's nerves, she told herself angrily. Nerves and resentment of his being away so much of the time. Claustrophobia. Leads to the screaming mimis.

She closed the dishwasher, pushed the "wash" button.

Frank?

He's all right, she insisted.

However, the feeling remained.

Chapter Two

"Mister," said the cabdriver, with obvious annoyance, "I've been driving a cab for eight years. If 621 West 93rd Street existed, here's where it would be. Between Broadway and West End Avenue."

Angrily, Frank leaned forward in the seat to catch the light from the street lamp onto the note he had scribbled before leaving his apartment. Yes, 621 West 93rd Street. And he hadn't even gotten her name!

"You want me to wait?" asked the driver.

"I not only wrote it down," said Frank, "I remember it. I remember her voice." With numbness bordering on quiet panic, he stared through the window at the not-quite-completed apartment building. The construction sign said it was a middle-income project. The whole Upper West Side was being redeveloped. There were many similar buildings, some occupied, some barely started. And how many individual small addresses had each swallowed up?

Okay. When he didn't show, she'd call back. Yeah, sure. *When?* Tomorrow?

Her name, her name! He had realized he didn't have it even before he reached his office, but at least he assumed he had the right address. If necessary—if it turned out to be an apartment building, he could have rung every doorbell.

The driver swung around, looked at him. "How long ago did you get the address? You know, it probably did exist—and would have been here, but they're tearing everything down."

Frank shook his head.

A couple walked by, arm in arm, and a dark-skinned man who looked drunk or drugged wove along slightly behind them. A woman, who seemed out of place because she was wearing a hat, walked toward the cab, hesitated, then came closer. She rapped on the window with her knuckles, and Frank jumped. It was eerie—almost dreamlike. Was she drunk? Her face looked late fifties, and the street light shadows sharpened her features into an almost surrealistic caricature, like a sculptured experiment in light and angles. Her eyes were hard to distinguish, but her lips formed a word—formed it twice before he understood. Klaner. His name!

Quickly, he rolled down the window.

"Mr. Klaner," she said, "I called you—"

His heartbeat quickened. He glanced at her hands. No brief case. A kaleidoscope of thoughts whirled through his brain. Wrong address. No brief case. Was she crazy?

He paid the driver, held tightly to her brief case and climbed out, slamming the cab door behind him. He was six foot one—maybe seven or eight inches taller than she. A cop strolled by on the other side of the street, and Frank found his presence reassuring.

"I'm terribly sorry," she said. She was wearing a nondescript gray coat, and it was still difficult to see her eyes. "My daughter's quite ill, and I haven't been able to think straight. I didn't realize until just a few minutes ago that I'd given you the wrong address. I did live here." She indicated the not-quite-completed vacant apartment building. "Before they tore it down. I lived here for almost thirty years."

He hesitated. Some of his doubts began to fade.

"I know I should have brought your brief case," she went on, "but I didn't think of it until I was almost here. I really am terribly sorry. I can't think any more. She's my only child."

"Huh? Who?"

"My daughter. She's critically ill."

Meaning it, Frank answered, "I'm sorry." He fell into step beside her. Garbage cans stood under street lights, and the sanitation department obviously did not work as hard on this side of town as on the East Side. This side was a mongrel. Bright, shining towers with terraces and picture window lobbies stood side by side with dark out-and-out slums. The weather was still cool enough that only a few stoop-sitters were out.

They continued on to 91st Street and Broadway, then turned the corner. On this block, 91st Street between Broadway and Amsterdam Avenue, the street lighting was inadequate and Frank's previous uneasiness returned. He told himself he was being silly. Her daughter was ill. She was reacting to this and he was reacting to her. He thought of Dianne, with her weirdo premonitions. Usually they were so poorly defined, it was virtually impossible to validate any of them. In addition, at that moment, he felt good—too good to let inadequate street lighting disconcert him. He'd been on a roller coaster of disappointment and hope that night, ever since he discovered the brief case was missing. Now the ride was almost over, and his nerves tingled—not unpleasantly.

"It's here," she said.

With an unusually sharp awareness of his surroundings, he looked at the building. It was a three-story brownstone, squatting between a semi-slum six-story building on the right and, on the left, a much higher new and far better kept apartment building. The brownstone had six stone steps leading to the front stoop. The bannister was stone with two medieval-looking stone lions, one on each side. The front door was bright orange, vivid even in the pale glow of a too-distant street light. A heavy brass lion's head door knocker whispered of other centuries.

"Place is pretty old, isn't it?" asked Frank. It was more of a remark than a question.

"Almost a hundred years," she answered. "One of the few survivors in this area." She reached into her oversize handbag and withdrew a key ring.

The hall, immediately beyond the door, was dimly lit and carpeted. The walls were paneled in dark wood, possibly mahogany, and the light came from what looked like a small antique lamp on a rococo-style table. The whole aura was one of splendor in a previous century, oddly depressing because the carpet was now worn through in spots, its once bright design now barely distinguishable. To the right was a staircase, also carpeted, but the carpet on the stairs was newer—and obviously cheap.

The woman turned right, inserted another key, then opened the door to her apartment.

Startled, Frank tried to keep his face straight and felt like a sonofabitch for wanting to laugh in the first place. The apartment was also dimly lit, but even in the dim light, he could see it was incredibly gaudy. The couch cover was splashed with the largest, brightest assortment of clashing flowers he had ever seen. The rug was patterned with wormlike curlicues of color, predominantly on a purple tone. A large fireplace dominated the opposite wall. Its overly ornate mantel supported four equally overly ornate apparently antique clocks. Four! And all had slightly different times. A bird cage hung near the heavily draped window, but the bird was nowhere in sight—hiding, perhaps. Framed photographs—possibly of relatives, ranged from faded tintypes to full-fledged modern, and decorated all three unmatched tables. The walls were adorned with four large oil paintings—one nude, one landscape, one vase of muddy flowers and one of a little girl, all apparently painted by the same obviously enthusiastic awful amateur artist. A wall mirror—in a chipped ornate gilded frame picked up a reflection of Frank beside the woman. Abruptly, she seemed poignant, partially due to the hat. A touch of splendor —a hat. She was dressed up. Or perhaps what struck him most strongly was the incongruity of her virtually colorless appearance against this outlandish backdrop.

She removed the hat. Frank was surprised. Her hair was gray and badly needed combing, but once upon a time, he realized, she must have been strikingly beautiful. The bone structure was still there—and the complexion.

For the first time, she smiled at him. "And now you must let me at least partially make up for all the trouble I've caused. Would you like a drink?"

"Huh? Oh. I mean, no. Thank you, but I have to get back to work." She *was* nuts, he decided. At least a little. Well, hell, the room showed that—showed that at least something about her was at least a little off.

"Well, goodness," she said. "Sit down. At least let me make you some coffee."

He wanted out. The room was beginning to grate on his nerves—not merely the clashing patterns and colors, but the quality—the aura of the whole building. "That's kind of you," he answered gently, "but, really—my associates are waiting for me," he lied. Associates. What an odd word for Frank to use—so—formal. The room was getting to him. Influencing his speech, for crissake—making it off center, not quite validly part of his real world.

Her reaction was subtle, but Frank felt somehow that she was disconcerted.

"Oh, please," she said. "Another ten minutes won't make any difference. I feel awfully guilty—not realizing I had the wrong brief case, then sending you to the wrong address. It's instant. I'll put the kettle on."

She walked out of the room, apparently toward the kitchen, still wearing her coat.

Frank hesitated, then—no. He was not going to stay. In addition to all its other negatives, the room was stuffy. And couldn't she even afford one decent lightbulb?

He started for the kitchen. The apartment was railroad lay-out. He followed the hall—carpeted and dimly lit. He passed four closed doors, two on each side.

He stepped into the kitchen and did a double-take. A large, orange, ceramic rooster decorated the window sill, and the wall was bordered by large flowers apparently painted by the same "artist" who'd done the oils in the living room. The stove looked like a fugitive from an antique shop, and the re-frigerator—well, at least it did not look as though the ice man still made regular appearances. The walls were pinkish orange except for a stark white replastered area near an electrical outlet apparently installed after the room had been painted.

"Miss—" he began awkwardly.

She jumped and swung around, almost knocking a cup onto the cracked and yellowed linoleum floor. "Oh!"

"I—I'm sorry," he said. "I really do have to go. If you'd just give me the brief case, I'd appreciate it."

She seemed more upset. She had removed her coat, and—surprisingly, her dress was also plain.

"Oh," she repeated. "Well, I mean, of course. But—" The water in the kettle started to boil, and a low whistle cut through the momentary silence between them. Her eyes were questioning.

"No," he answered, showing his irritation for the first time and beginning not to give a damn.

"All right," she answered quietly.

What the hell was she so edgy about, Frank wondered. His earlier sense of something not-quite-right returned—sharply.

She held out her hand toward the hallway that led back to the living room.

"After you," he answered softly, startled by the realization that he was on guard against her. It was okay, though. The gesture might be interpreted as mere courtesy. And yet—she seemed afraid of him. Afraid—of *him?*

Don't even try to figure it out. Fresh air—that was the main thing he wanted. That and his brief case.

"Wait in the living room," she said. "I'll get it for you."

He rested his eyes on the fireplace. It seemed the only area in the room where eyes could rest, and even the fireplace contained an overly ornate poker and andirons. A door in the hallway behind him opened. He turned and looked up—then, abruptly, looked down.

"Hi." It was a very small, female voice.

In spite of himself, he smiled. The voice belonged to a little girl, maybe four or five years old. A beautiful little girl with copper blond hair and deep blue eyes. She wore a floor length cotton nightgown.

"Hi," answered Frank.

A shriek, almost hysterical in pitch, "Get back into your

room!" It was the woman. She grabbed the child and virtually threw her behind one of the doors. The child screamed, the door slammed and Frank listened, stunned, as a key turned in the lock. The child continued to scream. The brief case—the woman had left it on the floor between the fireplace and the hall entranceway when she grabbed the child. Okay. Tell Dianne, he thought. Maybe the woman was really nuts. Maybe some agency should look into it. She'd mentioned a daughter— maybe the child was her grandchild. Poor kid. Stay out of it. The time was wrong.

He lifted the brief case as the woman returned to the living room. The brief case, his brief case, the feel of it was right. The weight, the way his hand fit the handle. A tremendous sense of relief—continuity, sanity—washed over him. He made a half turn toward the door. With slashing suddenness, his body stiffened, fingers spread, the brief case fell to the floor. Pain, sharp, searing, the side of his head. Everything went out of focus. Flashes of black and gray and color—every conceivable color spit before his eyes.

Awkwardly, yet rigidly, his face a mask of confusion, pain and disbelief, he turned, looked at the woman. Their eyes met. In her eyes, Frank saw terror—awake, alert. In her right hand was the brass-handled poker from the fireplace, her arm tentatively raised—again? Hit him again?

"My God," he whispered.

He took a step toward her—an uncontrolled, unplanned nerve reaction—then fell. Again, pain. Incredible, unbearable pain, as his head hit the marble hearth. He closed his eyes, the supreme triumph of conscious will. Some now-damaged pathway within his brain told him he was back in the army and to close his eyes so they'd think he was dead.

His body, of its own accord, went suddenly limp. Unconsciousness prevailed.

Slowly, tentatively, Amanda Hilton lowered the poker.

"Mr. Klaner—" she whispered. Awkwardly, trembling with fear, she dropped to her knees and reached under his coat and suit jacket—placed her hand over his heart. It was still beating.

Hysteria welled inside of her. What if he died? But he was supposed to die—only not like this. Her head ached and her body was covered with sweat. She looked at his face. It was abnormally white, eyes closed, mouth open, breathing shallow. There was blood on him—him, the rug, the hearth and the poker. There wasn't supposed to be any blood. None of it was supposed to be like this. He was supposed to have taken something to drink. A controlled, safe, drug-induced unconsciousness.

She thought of Sarah, her grandchild. Sarah had seen him. Amanda's fault. Amanda so rarely used the lock on the child's door. She had not turned the key properly.

Well, a four year old could easily be confused. However, Amanda should not have lost her temper. Now Sarah would be far more likely to consider the memory important.

But—more than that, could Sarah know who he was? Oh, not consciously, but—with feelings?

Still badly shaken, Amanda went into the bathroom. It was a large room, complete with peeling-paint linen closet and badly chipped tiles. The antique tub stood on small ornate feet, and the toilet had a pull chain.

Amanda opened the oversize medicine cabinet above the basin and removed the necessary first-aid equipment.

Fighting nausea, she tended to Frank's cut head. Blood—his head, her fingers, the bandages.

Finally, weakly, she rose to her feet, lifted one of his arms and pulled.

Nothing happened.

Whatever color had remained in her face drained out of it now. Certainly she had expected him to be heavy—but not this heavy. Motivated by near panic, she tried again, this time holding his ankles. She tugged and strained until her entire body seemed one enormous throbbing ache. Dropping his legs, she stood over him, breathing hard, and looked down. Tears flooded her eyes, blurring his image, his face, his coat. Then—yes! His coat! Its texture was rough, against a rough-textured rug.

Wrap a bed sheet around him, between the coat and the rug. A sheet, and a pillow for under his head. Heaven only knew, if she dragged him down all those stairs to the sub-basement with nothing protecting his head, he probably would be dead by the time she got him into the cage.

Chapter Three

✿✿*

The doorbell rang.

Dianne Klaner put down the sponge with which she had been wiping the sink, then dried her hands on a paper towel. "Who is it?" she called.

"Nancy."

"Nancy!" Surprised and delighted, Dianne opened the door. Nancy was Dianne's sister, two years younger than Dianne and a hard-core upstate suburbanite, rarely in the city.

"Hi," said Nancy, looking downright chic in spite of the fact that she, also, had two small children. "I would have called you, but the whole thing's last minute. We went out for dinner with one of Bill's clients, and the guy got smashed, so Bill took him home." Closing the door behind her, she added, "Got some coffee?"

"Sure."

Nancy followed Dianne into the kitchen and sat on one of the stools while Dianne ran tap water into a kettle. Almost compulsively, Nancy continued, "His wife's leaving him."

Dianne laughed. "You're impossible, Nancy. Who's wife is leaving who? Whom?"

"This *guy*. Bill's client. And he may lose his job too. Bill had no idea. He's one of these guys who never shows what he feels—you know, looks calm through any storm except that he chain smokes, drinks maybe a couple too many at lunch. He'll probably die when he sobers up and remembers everything he said. Both of us kept trying to stop him."

"Well, if he had to spill it out to somebody," answered Dianne, "be glad he picked somebody as nice as Bill. Here's your coffee."

"Thanks." They settled themselves comfortably in the living room, Dianne on the couch, Nancy on a chair near the window. "I feel so sorry for him," continued Nancy. "I guess you never really know what's inside somebody."

"Even somebody you think you know well—or think you *used* to know well," added Dianne, abruptly thinking of Frank.

"I'm sorry," said Nancy. "I haven't seen you in ages, and here I go on and on about somebody you've never even met. Where's Frank?"

"Who knows? Off playing with one of his nasty little computers."

"Don't knock it," said Nancy. "Just remember that awful little walk-up apartment you two lived in before he got interested in computers."

"I'm not knocking it. I mean, not really—I guess. It's just —oh, forget it. I'm in a mood."

"Why? What's wrong?"

Something inside Dianne snapped. "I want my husband, that's what's wrong. I married him because I wanted to be with him—I wanted to be his wife, but to me, 'wife' means more than a comfortable old chair you come back to after a long day's work."

Startled, Nancy answered, "Hey, *woah,* come on—how long has this been going on?"

"What? The resentment? I don't know. It started gradually, I guess. But"—she sat up, leaned forward on the couch—

"Nancy, I feel like I hardly even know him any more. What you said about that guy you and Bill were with tonight—how Bill had no idea what was going on inside him—I feel that way about Frank, too much of the time. I get little indications when he's under unusual pressure, but he so rarely talks to me any more. I sometimes feel it's because what he's doing is so complicated and technical and moving so fast he feels I wouldn't understand and he's just too tired to get into long explanations, but—I mean, what *am* I to him? And maybe the worst part is, I still love him," she added quietly. "I love him so much I sometimes want to call him up and drag him out of one of his damn conferences just to tell him so. And other times—I think, am I kidding myself? *Do* I love him? Is there really anything left?"

It was a long time before Nancy answered. Then, "Dianne, I'm so sorry."

Lips trembling, Dianne leaned her head against the back of the couch and closed her eyes. "Yeah. So am I. Honestly, I don't think I'm looking for Prince Charming. If I weren't married to Frank, I don't think I'd want to be married. I think I'd just—live here, with the kids. Go back to work. And sometimes when I think of the kids, I ask myself, isn't a very, very part-time father better than none at all except on alternate weekends or whatever it would be—and the answer is, I don't think it would really make much difference."

"Have you told him how you feel?" asked Nancy.

"I don't *know* how I feel. I'm all mixed up. I'm off again on again gone again. The only thing I know for sure is that most of the time, I'm unhappy. And lonely. And it's not the kind of loneliness you solve by joining committees or taking a course somewhere. I want my husband, darnit. I don't mean I want to own him—crawl around inside him—but I'm not the kind of wife who can just spend the money, care for the kids and be happy. Nancy, there was a time when if anybody had asked me who my best friend was, I'd have said Frank. You don't have to spend every waking minute being with and talking to your best friend—it's a feeling. A special kind of closeness. And if I can't have it with my husband, I don't want a husband. And if I were no longer married to Frank—this off again on again business—it would be *off*. I wouldn't be vulnerable to him."

"Of course you would. At least for a long, long time afterwards." Hesitantly, Nancy added, "Dianne, I think you—ought to talk to someone."

Dianne smiled. "Thanks. I just have—you. And I feel a lot better. I mean it—thank you."

"No, I don't mean me. I mean—a professional."

"Marriage counselor?" Thoughtfully, she continued, "I don't know. Maybe we should. I do love him, darnit. And there are rare moments—like a few minutes earlier tonight, when I get the oddest feeling that the emotion might be mutual."

"No, I don't mean that kind of a professional. I mean—look, I *know* you'll think it's silly."

"What?"

"Well, I mean somebody who—" She hesitated, gathered a little more courage, then continued, "Somebody who could tell you what the future would be if you did stay with him—or leave him."

"The *future?* Oh, for—" She laughed. "Nancy, come *on,* will you?" She sat up, feet firmly on the floor and took a pack of cigarettes from her shirt pocket.

"Just don't laugh, okay?" answered Nancy.

Gently, Dianne answered, "I'm sorry."

"And *that* was patronizing. I'm only trying to help."

"I know you are. And I am grateful—really. It's just—well,

honey, it *is* funny. I tell you I'm practically flipping my lid, and you tell me to go to a—a fortuneteller."

"That is *not* what I said."

"Okay." With controlled sibling irritation, Dianne continued, "I misunderstood you. What did you say?"

"Forget it, okay?" Then, "No, I changed my mind. Don't forget it. And don't say 'fortuneteller.' That makes it sound like a game. What I'm talking about is a psychic."

"And what, pray tell, is a psychic?"

"Well, it's a—" Lamely, she concluded, "a sort of *modern* fortuneteller."

Gently, Dianne answered, "Nancy, you are my sister and I love you, but honey, you are a kook—an absolute kook and always have been."

"There is nothing kooky about believing in ESP."

"Extra Sensory Perception. Knowing things beyond what our five senses tell us. It's a very scientific-sounding phrase."

"Why did you shudder?"

"Did I shudder?"

"You don't want to believe," answered Nancy, the tone of her voice accusing.

"Okay. I confess. You got it out of me."

"Dianne, it's like—well, like most of us are born with just AM reception, but occasionally somebody comes along who's got full-fledged FM. They can tune in on—well, signals the rest of us don't even know exist."

"Nancy, this conversation is ridiculous. I am not going to base my life—a decision as major as whether or not to stay with my husband, on what some two-dollar gypsy tea-leaf reader decides to tell me, probably depending on what she had for breakfast that morning."

"Not two dollars. Twenty. For forty-five minutes. And not

E. R. H. S.

'she.' 'He.' And he's not a gypsy, and he doesn't read tea leaves. He's a professional psychic. He uses ESP to help people."

"Good Lord. You know somebody."

"Well, as a matter of fact—"

"No!"

Intently, Nancy leaned forward on the chair. "Dianne, he told me about the house we lived in on Camedon Drive. He described the living room! He knew about Larry. Remember Larry Mangus? He took me to the high school Junior Prom. He died in Vietnam about two years ago. And remember when Bill was in that absolute turmoil on whether to go with another firm? He said Bill should go, and he was absolutely right! Dianne, almost six months ago, he said Bill would be invited to go into politics, and lask week, it happened. They asked him to run for the town council."

Wearily, Dianne answered, "Honey, I was not there. I do not know what was said or how he may have found out these things. I do know it doesn't take much intelligence to guess that a lawyer will be invited to run for something."

"Okay," said Nancy. Hurt mingled with anger. "Never mind. I just thought he might be able to help you, that's all."

Dianne rose to her feet, feeling even more keyed up than she had felt before Nancy arrived. "This is your fault," she said to Nancy, lightly. "You and your ESP. I was upset before you came, and now I'm a mess. Frank. Something to do with Frank."

"Huh?"

"I don't know. All evening I have had the darndest feeling that Frank was—I don't know. Danger. And now you make me wonder whether there's anything to it, when I know there isn't. I'm just lonely—hurt, I suppose, because we were going to have dinner together tonight, and then he walked out—on me. Office, again."

Seriously, Nancy asked, "What kind of danger?"

"I don't know. Something to do with a child. There—you figure it out. But don't lose any sleep over it, because by the time Frank gets home tonight, I'll probably feel like an idiot for having mentioned it. Come to think of it, I don't even know what time to expect him. What time is it now?"

Nancy looked at her watch. "Almost ten. I told Bill to pick me up here."

The phone rang. Dianne made a run for it, caught it on the second ring before it awakened Jimmy, asleep now in the dining-alcove bedroom next to the kitchen. "Hello?"

"Dah-anne? This is Pete Marshall. How are you?"

He didn't really need to give his name. She recognized the voice by the faint southern drawl, combined with the eternal careful courtesy of asking how she was. The *boss's wife*. "I'm fine, Pete. Frank's not here."

"Oh. Well then maybe you could help me."

The downstairs buzzer sounded.

"Hold on a sec," she said. Her hand over the mouthpiece, she called as quietly as possible, "Nancy, will you get it?" Then, back into the receiver, "Sorry. Someone at the door."

"Well, this'll just take a minute. Frank had a little trouble with his brief case, and—"

"It's okay," she interrupted. "He got it back."

"Oh. Well, I certainly am glad to hear it. Thank you, Dah-anne. Sorry I bothered you."

"It's all right. Good night." She hung up.

Nancy came into the kitchen, fresh from the intercom speaker in the hall. "Bill's here," she said.

"Okay. Please open the door so he won't ring the bell. If

Jimmy wakes up, I can't safely go to bed until he's asleep again, and heaven only knows when that'll be."

"You need a larger apartment—one with a full-size bedroom for him, close to your bedroom. Actually, a house would be better."

"Sure. Aside from the fact that we can't afford it, add at least two hours a day commuting time, and I might just as well forget I have a husband."

The doorbell rang.

"Darnit!" said Dianne.

"Oh gosh," said Nancy. "I'm sorry!" Quickly, she stepped out into the foyer and opened the door.

Bill looked tired. He was tall, brown hair, grayish brown eyes—almost ten years older than Nancy. Her semi-daddy—adoring, intelligent, calm and kind.

Dianne smiled. "Hi."

"Hi." He stepped inside. "Frank here?"

Dryly, Dianne answered, "Frank who?"

"Ouch. Wrong question. Come on, Nanc. I've got to get up at 6:00 A.M. tomorrow."

"Mommy—"

Dianne closed her eyes, felt irritation wash over her.

"Oh no," said Nancy. "Dianne, I'm sorry."

Bill looked confused.

"It's okay," said Dianne. "Really—I mean it." She scooped a sleepy-eyed Jimmy into her arms, held him close against her.

Coat slung over her shoulders, purse in hand, Nancy added, "Well—good night. And, Dianne—please think about it, okay? Just think about it."

"Huh?" She remembered. The fortuneteller. At twenty bucks a clip, no less. "Okay. Sure. I'll think about it."

"No, you won't," answered Nancy, almost petulantly. "You're very stubborn, Dianne. Do you know that?"

Bill opened the door and looked at his wife. "This way— all aboard."

"Bill, this is important!" snapped Nancy. "It's about Mark Hembric."

"Oh, Mark Hembric is important," answered Bill, dryly. To Dianne, he added, "Confidentially, I think she's in love with him."

"That's not true!" exploded Nancy. The force of her reaction startled Dianne.

Gently, Bill said, "Take it easy, Nanc. You are attracted to this guy—which I'll admit is probably one of the biggest reasons I don't like him."

"He married?" asked Dianne, for no reason in particular.

"No," answered Bill.

"You're jealous." Nancy smiled, but some of the lightness seemed forced.

"No," said Bill, "not seriously. I'm merely aware of the fact that in some areas, my lovely child bride, you are incredibly naïve. And from what you've told me of the psychic Mr. Hembric, I can only conclude that he is one slick operator."

Curiously, Dianne asked, "Have you met him?"

"No. And I have no desire to." Again, he looked at his wife and nodded toward the door. "Let's go, okay?"

She grinned. "Yes, counselor. Good night, Dianne."

Dianne smiled. "Good night." She waited until they were gone, then carried Jimmy, now heavy in her arms, into his bed.

"Wanna drink of water," he said, abruptly discouragingly wide awake.

"All right," answered Dianne, tiredly. "You stay here." She walked into the kitchen and filled a glass.

She hesitated, then left the glass on the sink and walked to the pad of phone numbers next to the telephone. Approximately three minutes later, Pete's familiar southern drawl was on the other end of the line.

"Pete, this is Dianne Klaner. Would you ask Frank to call me as soon as he arrives? Huh? Oh—no. It's not an emergency. I—" Awkwardly, she concluded, "I'd just like to hear from him, that's all. Thank you."

Chapter Four

Slowly, painfully, Frank Klaner regained consciousness. He lay on his back, surrounded by pitch blackness. Odors—damp, musty. Sound—a steady hum, like some large distant hovering insect. With trembling hands, he touched the primary source of the pain—the side of his head. Cloth. Gauze? Tape? Bandage.

He remembered, now. She had hit him with a poker. A *poker!* He had half turned—seen her face, only now the face was no longer hers. It was a caricature of every grade B horror movie he had even seen.

His definition of "pain" expanded. Other hurts which he had considered painful were now reclassified as "severely uncomfortable."

The complete blackness of his surroundings was disorientating. He started to stand, feeling somehow that he must consciously keep track of where the floor was.

He was unable to stand. Something held him back—a weight, a pressure around his left ankle. He leaned forward, feeling as though he might vomit, and checked the ankle. Disbelief washed over him, denied the evidence of his senses. A *chain?* He lifted it, felt the weight and texture of it, then dropped it, heard the clank echo through the blackness. A heavy-linked slightly rusted chain attached to a solid cuff which was clamped shut around his left ankle.

Frantically, angrily, he followed the chain to its source—a metal loop imbedded in a bricklike wall.

Slowly, heart pounding, he sank to a sitting position, leaned against the wall. Instinctively, he reached for his watch and the realization that he was unable to see it—or anything else —evoked rage. How dare she! That raving psycho had stolen his brief case, injured him with a poker, chained him—where?

A basement. That much was reasonably obvious. A basement on 93rd Street. No—91st Street. Five-eleven West 91st Street. An old brownstone with stone lions flanking a bright orange door.

He searched for a match. Each movement was painful. What the hell had she done to him—beaten him while he was unconscious?

Then—no. She had not beaten him. He was in a basement. She had probably dragged him down a flight of stairs to get him there.

He checked his pockets—coat, jacket, trousers—and found one pack of matches. By touch, there in the blackness, he counted—four matches. How much light—how much opportunity to take stock of his surroundings would four matches give him? A glorious two minutes, maybe. Certainly not much more.

Frantically—and unsuccessfully, he searched for another pack.

He wanted a cigarette. In that instant, almost as badly as he wanted his freedom, he wanted a cigarette—and dared not waste a match lighting it. Then, to hell with it. He found the cigarettes—how many cigarettes? He counted them, again by touch, and the sensation was eerie. He kept losing track. Then, finally, eight. Four matches, eight cigarettes.

With trembling hands, he placed a cigarette between his lips and struck a match.

The flame never touched the cigarette. Instead, he merely held it, enveloped by dreamlike disbelief.

Bars! There in front of him, maybe two or three feet away. Like a cell. He was in a jail cell, a cage!

The flame stung his fingers. Instinctively, he dropped the match. It was out before it hit the floor.

Trembling, aching, he pulled himself up onto his knees. With rigid control, he took his handkerchief and maybe ten or fifteen bottom sheets from the notepaper pad in his wallet. He scrunched up the paper, laid the handkerchief on top of it on the floor, then added his tie.

He lit the match. Cigarette, first. With closed eyes, he drew the smoke deeply into his lungs. It irritated his throat and made him dizzy, the dizziness probably largely due to the fact that he had had very little lunch and no dinner.

Quickly, while the match still burned, he touched it to the scrunched up notebook paper. Almost immediately, the paper flared into flames, tempered and kept alive by the handkerchief and tie. He half turned in both directions, as though trying to see everything all at once. A kaleidoscope of dancing shadows filled the room—the cage.

Yes—bars. Directly in front of him. A door with a keyhole that seemed almost a parody, made to take some giant, other-century, cast-iron key. More space beyond the bars—maybe five feet to the opposite wall. On the opposite wall, a fantastic assortment of apparently antique chains, handcuffs and locks hung from a long, horizontal row of hooks. The area behind the bars—where Frank was, was maybe ten by twenty feet, difficult to gauge because the boundaries were washed in flickering blackness. To his right was a screen beside a massive carved ornamented table and chair, which might have been selected by the same person who selected the stone lions by the front door. Briefly, strangely, he felt as though he had stepped backward in time—perhaps even a hundred years.

The flame was almost gone. Darkness washed in again. Instinctively, he touched his shirt. Wash and wear—would it burn or melt. Melt, probably.

Flickering light, dying. Then—again, light, but steady this time. A vague, pale rectangular spot of light on the floor, outside the cell.

Disorientated, queasy and still aching, he followed the line of the light—looked for its source. The ceiling? Yes. A rectangular opening in the ceiling outside the cage.

The flame was gone, now. Only the slightly stifling odor of smoke and a rapidly dying reddish glow remained.

He continued to look at the ceiling beyond the cell. The opening was small—maybe nine by twelve inches, but size was hard to gauge because distance distorts and he did not know how high the ceiling was. A light in a room above this room? A light which had not been there before. *Ergo,* someone had turned it on.

He held his breath. The distant buzzing sound became the only sound. Then—instinct or sound? Instinct, hell. Sound. Like metal hitting, scratching against metal. A key? Where? Where was the entrance way into the other part of the house?

He ground out the cigarette and lay down again, his face away from the bars.

Then—shades of a radio show suddenly disentombed from a menagerie of childhood memories—Inner Sanctum. The squeaking door. Like fingernails on a blackboard, the sound grated against his nerves. He lay very, very still.

Carefully, Amanda Hilton entered the room. Of course it

was unnecessary to really worry. He was not only locked inside the cage, he was chained. She carried a flashlight which was lit and an antique lantern which was not lit. Her first sensual impression as she entered the room was the faint odor of smoke—something burning?

Uncomfortably, she swung the flashlight beam into the cage. There he was. Her heart pounded. She kept the light pinned on him. He made no movement. Was he—still unconscious? No! Because she had left him on his back with his face exposed and he was now lying on his belly, face hidden.

Distastefully, she again sniffed the air. Yes, smoke. Good heavens, was he building fires in there? With the barely adequate ventilating system she'd rigged up, he'd suffocate himself. Well, all right. Let him. Heaven only knew, she still ached from dragging him down all those stairs. From the kitchen to the basement then basement to sub-basement, his hands and feet securely tied in case he awakened too soon.

She took a deep breath, moistened her lips and steadied her hand which held the flashlight.

"Mr. Klaner—"

Involuntarily, his muscles tightened at the sound of her voice. She's insane, he thought. He felt suspended in limbo.

Her voice firm, yet detectably nervous, she plowed onward, "Mr. Klaner, I know you're awake. Now if you intend to just lie there and not even give me the courtesy of an answer, I'll leave."

Courtesy? It was like a play. A satire, a parody. He rolled onto his back. The chain on his ankle gave a slight clank as several links changed position on the concrete floor. Squinting into the glare of her flashlight, he answered, "What do you want?"

Amanda drew herself up to her full five feet five inches,

not realizing that the light so blinded him he could barely see her. This was The Moment. With firm, quiet dignity, she answered, "I am Miriam Hilton's mother."

The name drew a complete blank. Still trying to define the image beyond the flashlight glare, Frank answered, "Miriam Hilton?"

"That's all right, Mr. Klaner. You have time to remember. Take all the time you need."

Something snapped. "Remember *what?*" he exploded, sitting up. "What the hell is this? Look, lady, in case you were unaware of it, it is illegal to go cracking people over the head and dumping them into—whatever the hell you've dumped me into."

"You have a very nasty mouth," she cut in, sounding far calmer than she felt. "You toss the word 'hell' around as though it were perfectly acceptable usage of the English language."

His mind went blank. No answer existed. Like trying to hold a coherent conversation with a cuckoo clock. Like one of those clocks on her living room mantel—four of them, each giving a slightly different time.

His headache was worse. Slowly, carefully, "Look, I'm sorry. I honestly don't know any Miriam Hilton. To the best of my knowledge, this is the first time I've ever heard the name."

"California, Mr. Klaner. About five years ago."

"Lady, I have never even been in—" He broke off. Yes, he had been in California—once. And, yes, it was about five years ago. A data processing convention. He'd gone with Pete Marshall and another guy from the office—Ed Lucas, a programmer. "Okay," he said. "Yes, I was in California about five years ago, but it was only for three or four days and I honestly, honestly do not remember any Miriam Hildon."

"Hilton," corrected Amanda, eyes blazing.

"Okay," Frank yelled right back at her, "but I *still* don't know her, goddamnit!"

"Wash your mouth out with soap!" spat Amanda. "When you do remember—a day, a week, a month—however long it takes, when you're ready to admit it, I'll bring you some food."

He was an animal, Amanda decided. Amanda was allergic to most animals. Of course, it was the fur—not the "aura" that made her sneeze. And he'd never be as dirty as a real animal—she hoped. After all, there was a toilet and wash basin behind the screen. Certainly—she hoped, he was human enough to take care of himself. "Good night, Mr. Klaner."

An answer froze in his throat. Not words—merely a sound, a vacuous protest.

She swung the light from his eyes, but he still could not see beyond lingering gray spots. Sounds—footsteps. The flashlight beam was to his left, now.

Metal clicked against metal. A key. Inner Sanctum again. *"Wait!"* he yelled.

Motion suspended. The only sound now, beyond his own heavy breathing, was the distant buzz he had grown used to before she arrived.

"I—" Lamely, impotently, he faltered. "Tell me what I'm supposed to have done."

The squeak resumed—loud, piercing, followed by a sharp, heavy clang. The door was closed, flashlight gone.

Instinctively, he turned his eyes toward the rectangle of light which came from the ceiling. Eleven o'clock. Pete. The computer site. His brief case. Dianne.

About a minute and a half later, the light disappeared.

Mouth dry, eyes wide, Frank stared into the surrounding, engulfing blackness. Silently, numbly, he wondered what she had in mind for him. He knew the answer. Hell, it was obvious. She intended to kill him.

Chapter Five

＊❖＊❖＊❖＊❖＊

Dreams. Images. A railroad track. No. Parallel lines. Geometric shapes. Dianne Klaner tossed restlessly in the shadowed psychic consciousness of early sleep. Parallel lines, rectangles. One of Frank's program charts—no, flow chart. That's what he called it. It was only the beginning of sleep. Thought patterns conditioned by conscious processes of logic reacted to the dream images. A flow chart—the flow of data, defined by a diagram. Parallel lines? No, not really. At least none of the diagrams Dianne had ever seen included lines like these. A bell, clanging, persistent—gone, then back again. The train whistle? The bell—ringing.

Abruptly, she opened her eyes—still not fully awake.

Oh, for—no, it was not a train whistle. It was the telephone on a small table beside the bed. As she lifted the receiver, she glanced at the luminous face of the clock radio on the same table. Eleven-twenty. Really only twenty minutes since she'd gone to bed?

"Hello?"

"Dah-anne? This is Pete. Hope I didn't wake you."

"Huh? Oh. Well, yes, but it's all right." She reached for the other bedside table, flipped on the lamp, then sat up. "What can I do for you?" she continued, closing her eyes against the light. Get used to it more gradually.

"Er—is Frank there?"

"No. At least, I don't think so. Wait a sec." She left the receiver on the bed and looked out into the hall.

"Frank?"

No answer.

She returned to the bed, again lifted the receiver. "No. I thought maybe he'd come in and I didn't know about it."

"Well—we're at D.S.I. and he was supposed to meet us here at eleven. You see, we're charged for use of the computer from eleven on, and we can't use it until Frank gets here because he's got what we need to work with in his brief case."

"Oh. Well, I'm sorry. Did you try his office?"

"Yes, ma'am."

"Oh. Well—I don't know. Maybe he got tied up in traffic or something." *Or something,* she thought. Stop it, she told herself angrily. It's nerves—being cooped up here so much of the time. Still, the fact remained, Frank was not where he was supposed to be and he had not called either Pete or Dianne.

"Well, okay," said Pete. "If you do hear from him, I'd appreciate your havin' him give us a call."

"Yes," she answered, uncomfortably wide awake now. "I will."

She replaced the receiver, then lit a cigarette. The worried little wife, she thought dryly. It was a game—one which would end, of course, as soon as she heard from Frank. Maybe she wanted to worry. Convince herself her feelings for him were still alive. No, more than just alive. Perhaps she wanted to care the way she used to, such a long, long time ago.

She ground out the cigarette, flipped off the lamp and pulled the covers up to her chin. It was lonely in bed without Frank, yet it was a kind of loneliness she was growing used to. Also, she was beginning to find it less and less unpleasant. The first few minutes were usually not easy, but the point was, she didn't *need* him. She was no longer upset by his absence. Merely a little lonely—a little sad, perhaps. But perhaps that, too, in time would pass. She closed her eyes. Did she want it to pass?

Oh, no-o-o-o! Not that merry-go-round again. Not tonight, thank you.

She closed her eyes.

Sleep.

"Mommy, Mommy!"

Dianne Klaner opened her eyes. Sunlight—sharp, stark. Morning? Of course it was morning. Strange—she felt almost drugged. No, it wasn't strange at all. She'd had very little sleep last night. Dreams. Smokelike images. Gone, now.

"Mommy," insisted five-year-old Tracy. "Get up! Jimmy got into the refrigerator and broke a jelly jar. I told him you'd be mad," she added with a trace of smugness.

Now the words penetrated. Broken jelly jar—broken glass, and a three year old dipping eager sticky fingers into that glass. Still not fully awake, she jumped to her feet and ran into the kitchen.

"Jimmy!"

The jelly jar was immediately visible. Jimmy was not. She looked under the table. Yes—there he was, his expression so innocent she laughed. No, she wasn't supposed to do that. She was supposed to be con-sis-tent. All the books said so.

She held out her hand. "Come on, Jimmy. Let's wash your face." Well, at least he was okay. If he'd cut himself, he'd be howling.

For the first time since she'd awakened, she thought of Frank. Strange—he wasn't in bed. Or was he? She'd been so sleepy—run out of the room so fast. To Tracy, she said, "Honey, will you help Jimmy wash his face?"

Still in her bare feet, wearing only a light cotton nightgown, Dianne walked back to the bedroom.

No, Frank was not there.

"Frank—" she called.

Tracy, holding Jimmy's hand and leading him toward the bathroom, answered, "Daddy's not here."

"Don't wanna get washed," announced Jimmy, suddenly breaking away from his sister.

"You get into that bathroom and wash your face!" exploded Dianne, startled by the shrillness in her voice. She looked at her watch and the time suddenly penetrated. Eight-fifteen. She'd never get Tracy over to the kindergarten class by eight-forty.

She grabbed the kitchen phone and called a neighbor. "Sally, it's a madhouse up here. Can you do me a favor and take Tracy to school this morning?"

"Oh. Okay. Sure."

Quickly, yet largely mechanically, Dianne dressed Tracy, shoes tied just as the doorbell rang.

After they left, Dianne stood in the kitchen and looked at the splattered jelly. It was—eerie, the way life continued, totally indifferent to the fact that Frank had apparently not come home last night. The broken jelly jar, kids fighting—even the way the sun poured into the apartment, warm and familiar. The cherry tomato plant on the window sill needed to be watered.

"Mommy—will you snap my jeans?"

She looked at her son. How like Frank he was—even the way he walked.

"Yes, dear," she answered softly. She snapped his jeans,

then gave him a quick hug, forcing herself to keep it quick. A flutter of quiet panic passed through her. This was real.

Eight-thirty. Another half hour before the switchboard at Frank's office opened. It wouldn't be the first time he had gone into the office early. It would be the first time he hadn't come home, though.

The computer place! That darned computer place was open twenty-four hours a day, seven days a week.

She started into the bedroom, then remembered the broken jelly jar. It was dangerous. Jimmy was liable to come back to it.

She cleaned the floor—and wall and refrigerator, then dried her hands and reached for the phone.

Sound—a loud clank from the bathroom, followed by running water. Nerves shot, she yelled, "JIMMY, GET OUT OF THE BATHROOM!"

He let out a yell. Crying again. He seemed to cry so much of the time, these days. Was it Dianne's fault? No—at least maybe not. He was almost four. The book said four was an awful age. Briefly, almost instinctively, she tried to remember Tracy at four, but was unable to concentrate.

She reached the bathroom and discovered the plastic drinking glass in the bathtub. The wash basin drain was closed, the water already beginning to flow onto the floor. One free-in-this-box-of-cereal plastic sea monster was just about to float over the edge. She grabbed the faucet handle, shut off the water and opened the drain.

Jimmy's crying told her he was in his room.

She closed her eyes and leaned against the bathroom wall. Jimmy was only a baby, she reminded herself, rigidly. And yet her frustration remained—thoroughly, painfully adult.

The phone rang.

She took it in the bedroom. "Hello?"

"Dah-anne?"

Pete! She sank onto the bed, still holding the receiver. Something was wrong—very, very wrong. "Yes, Pete—"

"Is Frank there?"

Numbly, she answered, "No."

"Have you heard from him?"

"No."

Slight pause. Then, in that same southern drawl—now minus the amenities, apparently through preoccupation, "We waited until midnight last night, then I canceled the machine time. I did leave word for him to call us—you and me."

"Pete, do *you* have any idea where he might be?"

This time, the pause was longer. "No," he said. "I thought you might."

"Maybe the office—" she offered lamely, not even believing it herself.

"Well, that's where I am," he answered.

She glanced at the clock radio beside the bed, then looked at her watch. Her watch had stopped. It was actually ten after nine. "I'd better—" The words trailed off. Call the police, she thought. The words seemed strange to her—almost as though they were part of a foreign language. "Did you speak to his secretary?" she said. "Maybe he—got in touch with her."

"Yes, ma'am. I did speak to her. Last time she saw him was late yesterday afternoon."

Dianne closed her eyes.

The TV blared on so loud that she almost dropped the phone receiver. The sound was incomprehensively distorted. "I have to go," she said. She slammed the receiver back onto the hook, then ran into the living room, grabbed the TV volume control and turned it down—way down.

Jimmy, perched on the back of the couch, cringed. "You gonna yell at me?" he asked.

With rigid control, she answered, "Jimmy, you may watch TV. Do not make it any louder." She should have thought of it earlier. Park him in front of the TV. Frank didn't want him to watch TV during the day, but Frank had no concept of what trying to watch him all day was like.

She walked back to the bedroom. Blame her slight dizziness on the fact that she hadn't eaten, blame the general sense of disorientation on the fact that it was nine-thirty and she wasn't dressed yet.

Mechanically, she sat on the bed, lifted the phone receiver and dialed "O" for operator.

The policeman's voice had a slight accent—Bronx, maybe. All the way from the Bronx to this Upper East Side precinct.

"My husband didn't come home last night," she said. Somehow it sounded awfully cliché.

"Hold on a sec," he answered. Then—same voice, "Okay."

Questions—methodical, courteous. When was he last seen? Had she checked his office? Where did he usually park his car? No car. Okay. Anything physically wrong—cardiac— diabetic—anything? Anyone who might want to hurt him? Anything missing that might indicate he disappeared by choice? "Well, look, I'll tell you what to do," he continued. "If you haven't heard from him by noon, check his office again and if they haven't heard, give us another call."

Numbly, she shook her head. He was wrong, this was serious. "No," she said, "please—something's happened to him."

"Well, maybe, but maybe not," he answered, not unkindly. "We get a lot of calls here and sometimes it *looks* like somebody's missing, but then they turn up, perfectly okay. You see, we don't have enough men to check out every call we receive. And that's why we like to be sure there really is a problem. Now if you don't hear from him by noon—"

Numbly, helplessly, Dianne answered, "All right."

She hung up.

It was eerie. She knew it was not "all right."

She looked around the room. Laundry to be ironed. Frank's non wash-and-wear shirts back from the Chinese laundry yesterday still had to be put away. The sun poured in onto the unmade bed, and a faint summer breeze stirred the curtains. How normal it all seemed.

At approximately eleven-forty, she returned from the kindergarten with Tracy. The day was beautiful—a day to let all except the basic housework go and sit in the park with the kids. Let them take off their shoes and run in the grass beside the fenced-in concrete play area. Soon the sprinklers would be turned on. Summer! That crazy, lazy not quite real time of year. Only three more weeks, and the schools would close for summer vacation.

When in the course of human events—the day by day by day course of small everyday human events—then, suddenly, everything goes completely haywire.

At approximately twelve-fifteen, Dianne parked both kids in front of the TV, walked into her bedroom at the other end of the apartment and called Frank's office. No, they had not heard from him.

She called the police.

Chapter Six

"Don't wanna go home!" protested Sarah Hilton, age four, to her grandmother, Amanda Hilton. The playground in the park at 93rd Street and Central Park West was crowded today, the weather exceptionally lovely. It was the kind of day Amanda loved best. Something about it—memories of her own life, a time when youth and summer belonged to her especially and most personally. A time when she had taken her own daughter, Miriam, to this very park. How like Miriam Sarah was—the same sunbeam-filled reddish blond hair, long, never remaining neat. The same wide deep blue eyes, slightly turned-up freckled nose. Except, perhaps, Sarah was prettier than Miriam. Amanda continued to look at her granddaughter, suddenly struck by the oddest sensation. Another child—also blond and around four years of age stood several feet behind Sarah, near the swings. Simply stood there, looking in Amanda's direction, holding a sand bucket and shovel. It was almost as though—Miriam had come back through time into this childhood instant to look at—even play with her own daughter.

Tears moistened Amanda's eyes. And yet, in a way, Miriam *was* still alive. Alive through Sarah.

Amanda smiled at her granddaughter. "Well," she said, "if we leave now, you'll have time for ice cream after lunch, before your nap."

Sarah hesitated. Then, "No!"

Amanda's lips tightened. Managing a four year old was not easy. High-spirited, that's what Sarah was. And stubborn. Like Miriam. Miriam had been extremely stubborn—and look where it got her! Amanda tried to feel angry, but the emotion of sorrow—as usual, washed it away. Sorrow. Pain. The two were so terribly intertwined. There were nights, even after all these years, when Amanda had to use sleeping pills to escape the wakefulness of active sorrow.

"Do you want to make Grandma feel bad?" she said. "Do you want to make Grandma cry?"

"No," answered Sarah, very quickly. She threw her arms around Amanda, and Amanda permitted herself the emotional luxury of holding her granddaughter close to her, but only for an instant. The child was filthy—covered with sand and dirt. If only children didn't get so dirty. If only—all of life could be even a little more orderly.

Abruptly, Amanda stood and took Sarah's small hand in hers. "Come, dear," she said. "We can come back again tomorrow, if you're a very good girl."

Sarah had no particular desire to be a very good girl—or even a moderately good girl, but her grandmother was big and warm and she liked the feel of Amanda's hand holding hers.

As they approached the house—the century-old brownstone with the orange door and stone lions, Sarah broke away from Amanda, ran in front of the house and growled at the lion on the left. Momentarily disconcerted, Amanda took quick control of herself. "Come along, dear," she said, unlocking the door. It was indeed a burden to care for Miriam's child, but there was no one else—for Sarah or Amanda.

They walked through the hall, over the faded and worn carpet, past the chipped, ornate ceramic lamp.

"Okay," called a female voice from the top of the stairs, "See ya."

Irritably, Amanda fitted her key into the lock on the door to the downstairs apartment.

Kathy Gillmore—age twenty-two, deep auburn hair and unbelievably green eyes, rushed down the stairs. An actress—or would-be actress—that's what Miss Gillmore was. There were three of them sharing that walk-up upstairs apartment. Amanda's great grandfather who'd built the house would hardly approve. Had Amanda known they were actresses, she would not have rented to them. The only one she had met before giving them the lease seemed sweet—worked in an office, then. Didn't mention she was in "show business." To Amanda, the phrase carried a circus connotation, loud and ridiculous.

Of course Amanda's great grandfather could not have foreseen the way prices and property taxes would rise. Nor could he have foreseen Amanda's husband walking out on her, almost thirty years ago, only to die six years later, leaving her with no insurance money.

But Amanda did not want to think about Miriam's father. Strange—in Amanda's mind, he had remained as young as that Mr. Klaner, even though she knew the years would have changed her husband as they had changed her. Time, lately, occasionally seemed out of focus to Amanda, confusing. She was fifty-eight—certainly not old, and yet, lately, there had been brief instances when she had felt much younger. Rooting around in the attic about six months ago, she found a dress she'd worn on her honeymoon. The oddest, most disorientating sensation took hold—as though, if she were to slip into that dress, everything around her would change back to the day she'd first worn it. And yet, at other times, she woke up afraid to look at her hands—as though, there in her bed in the morning sunlight, her hands would suddenly appear gnarled and withered, and Sarah would be all grown up— and gone.

Kathy Gillmore gave one quick acknowledging nod to Amanda, then walked out, slamming the door behind her. The slam set Amanda's teeth on edge, in anger.

Amanda opened the door into her lower-floor section of the house. Sarah dashed in ahead of her, then stopped—abruptly, in the entrance way between the living room and the long corridorlike hall.

"He stood here," she announced.

Some of the color left Amanda's face. Quickly, she closed the door to the outside hall. "No, Sarah," she said. "I told you, that was something you dreamed. To keep talking about it is telling a lie."

"I'm *not* lying," insisted Sarah. "He had black hair and he was nice. He smiled at me."

"Do you know what happens to liars?" exploded Amanda. "Their tongues shrivel up, and they can't talk!" No, that was the wrong thing to say. Now Sarah was more likely to remember.

Confusion mingled with melting determination. "I think he was here," answered Sarah.

Amanda smiled, but her eyes remained frightened. "Of course he was, darling. And he gave you candy and potato chips and he had a cape, like Superman."

Sarah tried to remember. She was not quite sure what "dream" meant. She knew it had something to do with sleep, but that was about all. Candy? Potato chips? Sarah knew where

Amanda kept the potato chips. She grinned. "Betcha can't eat just one!" she cried. Abruptly, she ran down the corridor to the kitchen.

After lunch—peanut butter and jelly sandwiches, which Amanda liked almost as much as Sarah, Amanda tucked Sarah into bed for a nap. On her way out of the child's bedroom—carefully, quietly, Amanda locked the door.

She returned to the kitchen.

Now! What food should she offer Mr. Klaner? She had not been down to see him since last night. Let him really feel hungry.

She tried to hate him, but her feelings were mixed. Even though Amanda had stopped going to church when her daughter died, the threads of a strict religious upbringing were still tightly woven within her. To hate was sinful.

Yet wasn't it God's will that she do exactly as she had done? For without God's help, how could she possibly have gotten Mr. Klaner into the cage?

Still preoccupied, Amanda opened the refrigerator door. *Vengeance is mine, sayeth the Lord,* she thought. Yet who was to say the Lord might not choose human hands to perform the mechanics of that vengeance?

She looked at the refrigerator shelves and shook her head. Next week, for sure, she must organize the contents of that refrigerator—dairy on one shelf, sweet things on another. There must be at least half a dozen jars of applesauce in there, each half empty.

Men. What did men like to eat? Her own husband had liked toasted cheese, but that wouldn't do here. In case Mr. Klaner continued to pretend he didn't know anything about Miriam, the cheese would grow cold and cold toasted cheese was practically inedible.

Oh, for heaven's sake, peanut butter and jelly would be fine. Certainly the least complicated to prepare.

She scooped the jelly onto the bread and realized her hands were unsteady. Had she merely dreamed all of it? No. And yet there were still times when she wondered. When she was with Sarah, she was all right—quite sure what was real, but when she thought of Mr. Klaner, the line between planning and actually carrying out those plans seemed awfully thin. She had planned with such intensity for such a long time and, in her planning, experienced emotions quite similar to the emotions evoked by the actual deed. The difference now —and she could not even say it was completely unanticipated —was that now her nerves seemed threaded to a higher pitch.

The main trouble was, she remembered, he had refused to drink anything last night after she got him into the house. She had had to hit him with a poker. What if—after she killed him, something else went wrong?

Angrily—almost as though talking to Sarah, she told herself to stop dwelling on the negative aspects. Her father had died of a heart attack, worrying about problems which, in the final outcome, proved to be relatively minor.

She packed the sandwich and one can of Diet Pepsi-Cola in a waxed garbage bag, then collected her flashlight and lantern. As soon as he decided to be honest with her, she would leave the lantern with him—leave him some light.

The keys were in an old copper canister, on which the letters COFFEE had almost completely worn off—in with about two dozen other miscellaneous keys and small objects. The particular set of keys leading to the cage were all on a dime-store chain. She took the chain, then inserted the shiny key into the relatively new lock on the door which led to the basement. She flipped on the overhead light and walked down the wooden stairs, periodically steadying herself with the help of the wrought-iron railing installed by her husband when the wooden railing, old and worn, developed splinters. Managing the flashlight, lantern, food and keys was awkward. In addition, the top step squeaked dreadfully, constantly threatening to break. She must remember to replace it, along with the burned-out lightbulb over the stairway area.

The basement was cluttered—a workbench which had once belonged to her husband, a faded upholstered chair with broken springs and the stuffing coming out, some miscellaneous lumber, one large steamer trunk, two smaller trunks, a now badly rusted stroller which she had used when Miriam was a baby.

She turned right, past the separate room which contained the furnace. This was where she'd first had trouble, after she read her great grandfather's diary and attempted to locate the sub-basement entrance. There had not even been a furnace room when the diary was written. It was quite a diary. She found it about six months after Miriam's death. Amanda was in the attic rooting through the accumulated family belongings of four generations, looking for storage space for some of Miriam's things, when the corner of an old steamer trunk smashed against one of the attic walls, revealing a hollow section behind the paneling. The hollow section contained the diary. Her great grandfather had built the cage shortly after the house was completed, almost a hundred years ago. Built it for an unfaithful wife who died, too soon, never even knowing it existed. There were still times, like this moment, when Amanda marveled at the ingenuity of the whole scheme. He absolutely could have gotten away with it, could have put his wife down there—his first wife, not the one who later bore his children. The whole idea was so outlandish, no one would ever have suspected. They'd all think she ran off with one of her lovers. They'd feel so *sorry* for him. The planning was brilliant. Sub-basements were not unheard of, and her great grandfather was an architect. He simply drew up a duplicate set of plans, after the house was completed, and the duplicate set showed only what he wanted known. By then, the men who'd actually built the house no longer remembered this house any more than any other house. The bars—and everything else which might have made this sub-basement memorable, he installed himself.

Her first impulse had been to sell the diary or give it to a museum. It was like a novel—the kind of novel she used to read when she was a teen-ager, yet this was so much more because it was real. The man had actually lived, breathed, thought and done these things, written them down. Reading it was like stepping into another life, another time. Now, of course, the man's passions were dead as he was dead, but the words in the diary were still alive and the cage still existed.

The door to the sub-basement was inside a storage closet. Such closets were common when the house was built. A later tenant had even replaced the closet door with a newer, sturdier door. Nothing secret, here. She used a second key and unlocked the storage closet.

The closet was almost a small room with floor to ceiling rows of heavy wooden shelves. Amanda still remembered her grandmother filling those shelves with lush home-canned fruits and jellies. Now, though, the shelves were practically empty. One bare lightbulb protruded from an electric light fixture in the middle of the ceiling. Amanda pulled the string, and the room flooded with light.

She closed—and locked, the closet door behind her. Ahead, to her right, she placed the sandwich bag, flashlight and lantern on the floor. With both hands, she lifted out the three lowest shelves. They were heavy, awkward and squeaked a bit but she managed, laid them aside.

Now the break in the cement wall was visible—the outline of a closed door, perhaps three feet by four. She released the bolt and pushed, with all her strength—outward, away from her. It squeaked, but not badly.

Light from the storage closet poured into the area beyond —an area not shown in the second set of architectural plans, but one which she knew had been discovered long after her great grandfather died because it contained a relatively modern electrical outlet. This area, quite cleverly Amanda thought, had been used to store wine—a logical reason for its secrecy in case it were discovered. When Amanda found it, four bottles of wine remained—bottles now stored in her kitchen, awaiting some tremendously special occasion.

She climbed through the three by four opening, then stepped down into the wine storage area. Here, this supposedly final floor of the building was in rectangular concrete blocks. This was where Amanda had the electric fan, plugged into the outlet a previous tenant had installed for light. The fan buzzed away—circulated and directed air through a hole previously occupied by one of the concrete blocks. Instructions for removal of the block had been included in the diary, set up on a leverage principle—not at all difficult.

A peculiar sense of depression—even fear, touched Amanda. Not even fear that something might go wrong. Rather, it was fear of death. As though, by causing Mr. Klaner's death, she would confirm her own mortality. And yet, hadn't Mr. Klaner killed Miriam?

She tried to imagine how she'd feel when it was over. Relief, that's what she'd feel.

She lifted four wine shelves from their proper slots—same principle as the storage closet entrance. Shelves now propped on the floor, Amanda faced the concrete door which led to the next flight of stairs. This door also opened outward, the hinges on the side with the lower stairs. It was a standard door—swung open to the side. Amanda inserted a large wrought-iron key into a keyhole previously hidden by one of the shelves. She opened the door, then—paraphernalia in hand, walked down the slightly curved flight of stairs to the last door—a huge iron door with a small barred window. This area was almost pitch black, except for the beam of Amanda's flashlight. Here, she used the next key. The door squeaked dreadfully—set her teeth on edge.

Now. She was in The Room. She stood near the faint rectangle of light from the wine storage area above and looked at the cage. Carefully—Amanda was extremely careful, she placed the unlit lantern and key ring on the floor by the wall far opposite the cage. Just in case—heaven forbid, he ever managed to get his hands on her, at least he would not be able to get the keys.

She beamed her flashlight into the cage. He was sitting up, way over in the corner, with his back to her. Hadn't even turned around when he heard her come into the room. Hateful, that's what he was! Hateful, crude, discourteous and foulmouthed.

Voice tight, she said, "Mr. Klaner—"

Chapter Seven

"I have never before felt so completely inadequate," said Dianne.

Her father listened, at a loss for words which might comfort his daughter. His wife, dead two years now, was the one who'd always found words.

Nancy sat back and lit another cigarette. It was Nancy who had suggested they meet in their father's apartment, where Dianne's children could not overhear. In addition, meeting somewhere other than Dianne's apartment meant Dianne had to get dressed. Again, Nancy surveyed Dianne's clothes—a simple beige sweater, amber beads and straight-line brown tweed skirt. Inappropriate, but Dianne did not know Nancy's plans for the evening went beyond a brief visit with their father. Inconspicuously, Nancy checked her watch. Almost seven-thirty. Still time to talk. Unlike their father, more like their mother, Nancy found words. "Well, now, come on, honey. You said they did check Missing Persons, all the hospitals, the—" She broke off. Wrong words.

"The morgues," concluded Dianne, dryly. "Then where is he?" Her voice cracked. "What if something did happen to him, but they just haven't found him yet? Nancy, I don't think they care. No, I take that back. They do care, but it's mechanical. They think—that if Frank's disappeared, it may be because he wanted to disappear. I talked to two detectives, and one of them in particular—I mean, I think he meant to be nice, but—twice, he said an adult male can usually take care of himself. And I know they have a lot of standard questions they probably ask everybody, but they kept trying to find out if—" Her voice trailed off, "If there might be another woman."

Incredulous, Nancy said, *"Frank?"*

"Well, how do I *know?*" exploded Dianne. "I told you, I see so little of him—feel so far away from him."

"Oh, come on. You'd know if your husband were seeing someone else."

"How? His hours are irregular. Two or three times a year he goes on out-of-town trips."

"Well, he wouldn't just—there'd be money missing—or something," she added lamely.

"That's what I've told myself," answered Dianne. "I know *I* couldn't just leave, but—Frank? I don't know. He's not exactly sentimental."

"Every man's sentimental," broke in her father. "It's a matter of degree. Look, Dianne, I have a little money. If you decide you want to hire someone—"

"Private detective," said Dianne. "Sam Spade. Mike Hammer."

Nancy bit her lip. No, this would not be the right time to say anything.

"Dad, I don't know," Dianne continued. "I did think of it. I thought of going to his parents. Heaven knows, they'd hire the best and never miss the money, no matter how much it cost. I'm just afraid of what the shock might do to them."

"Huh?" said Nancy.

"Oh, you know. His father's had two heart attacks in the

last year and a half. His mother's practically living on tranquilizers. Look, Dad, let me think about it. I want to double-
check everything myself, first. Maybe *I* could come up with
something to give the police—something to indicate that he
didn't just walk out voluntarily. And on the other hand, if
there is another woman, with a private detective asking questions all over the place—going into this whole thing much
more deeply than the police have—well, I'm just afraid it would
get back to the kids. How do you explain to children that
Daddy didn't even love you enough to say good-by?"

"But you don't really believe it is another woman," said
Nancy.

"I repeat, how would I know? Sex? No change there, but
—no. You're right, I don't believe it's another woman. I just
feel so—oh, Nancy, remember what I said about not being
sure I wanted to stay with him. But—this. I mean, if we were
separated"—she forced herself to say the word—"divorced,
okay, we wouldn't be together, but at least I'd know he was
all right, I'd know he wasn't alone or hurt or sick or—"

Gently, her father cut in, "Sounds like you love him."

"I think I do," answered Dianne. "Sometimes. Maybe I
just don't want to."

"But you do want to know where he is—now—" said Nancy.

Startled, Dianne answered, "What kind of a question is
that?"

Gathering all her courage, Nancy said, "Dianne, I want
you to meet Mark."

"Mark? I—oh, for heaven's sake!"

Nancy leaned forward in her chair and continued, quickly
—too quickly. "Dianne, please don't think I'm crazy. Don't
laugh at me like Bill laughs. Remember Bill said he thought
I was in love with Mark? Sure, he was half kidding, but only

half. Dianne, *this* is why Bill's so down on Mark. I tell you Mark—knows things. Things nobody could know unless they really did have a gift. A very special gift, Dianne."

"Well, Bill's certainly right about one thing," snapped Dianne. "You're twenty-six years old, Nancy, but you're a baby!"

"Hold it," cut in their father. "Who's Mark?"

"Mark Hembric," answered Nancy, quickly. "He's a professional psychic. And I honestly, honestly believe he could help you, Dianne. Look, tonight he's going to be right near you—I mean, it would be easy to get to. An apartment on Sutton Place."

"Sutton Place?" answered Dianne. "My goodness, your Mr. Hembric certainly doesn't mess around with the lower echelons, does he?"

"Like everyone else, he has to earn a living," she answered defensively. "And just because someone has money doesn't mean they don't also have problems."

"Does he tell them which stocks are going up?" asked Dianne dryly.

"No. Because that would be illegal. In New York, it's illegal to tell the future. Besides, any honest psychic will tell you, the future is not preordained. Only *tendencies*—what's *likely* to happen. But we're not talking about what *may* happen with Frank, you want to know what *has* happened."

"No," said their father to Nancy. "I know you want to help, but this is wrong."

"Can it hurt?" she asked defiantly.

"Yes. When your brother died—way back when you were little kids, your mother started going to mediums. I finally had to stop her because of the money, but—honey, it kept the grief alive. I know she would have accepted his death much sooner if she hadn't felt she could still communicate with him."

Startled, Nancy answered, "You never told us."

"Why should I? You kids accepted his death. Why prolong it for you?"

"Mark is not a medium," answered Nancy. "He deals only with psychic sciences. Astrology, palmistry, telepathy, clairvoyance, radiaesthesia—"

"Radia—*what?*" asked Dianne, unimpressed.

"Discovering things otherwise unknown by use of an object. Like a divining rod to locate water or a swinging pendulum to answer questions."

"Oh, for—" In spite of her annoyance, Dianne laughed. "Can't you just picture this guy wandering all over the country looking for Frank with a divining rod?"

"Stop it," snapped Nancy, close to tears now.

"Tell me," said Dianne, "how does your Mr. Hembric reconcile this can't-tell-the-future idea with people like Jeane Dixon? After all, she predicted—"

"Kennedy's assassination," finished Nancy. "No, she did not! If you look at what was written *before* the assassination, you'll find that all she said was that whoever was elected President in 1960 would either be assassinated or die in office. And in view of the fact that every President elected in a year ending in zero since William Henry Harrison *has* died in office, it was a pretty unimpressive guess. It was a tendency, Dianne. An unchecked tendency which, therefore, came true. And I'll tell you something else. Her prediction on who would win that Kennedy-Nixon election was *Nixon,* not Kennedy. Now, maybe this also was a tendency—but a tendency that was checked. And this is what Mark does. He can tell you tendencies—what's *likely* to happen if you—well, just let things drift."

"So that explains Jeane Dixon's goofs," said Dianne. "And Mark Hembric's."

"Mark is incomparably more accurate than Jeane Dixon. Jeane Dixon happens to have a name, but there are thousands of even amateur psychics far, far more gifted, more psychic, more accurate than Jeane Dixon. Dianne—this thing tonight —it's a group. Maybe twenty people in an apartment. It's— well, it's for fun. He reads minds. Maybe somebody will give him an object, and he'll talk about the person who owns or did own it, even though he's never met them. But—honey, it'll show you some of what he can do."

"He's not going to show me anything, because I'm not going."

"I already spoke to him about you. I asked whether I could bring you tonight. He got special permission from the hostess."

"You never give up, do you?" Dianne lifted her handbag from the coffee table, rose to her feet. "Good night, Dad."

"Good night, honey. Now, Nancy, take it easy—"

"All right," said Nancy. "Good night, Dad."

Their father out of sight now, Nancy and Dianne walked to the elevator. "He said something about you," offered Nancy.

Wearily, Dianne answered, "Nancy, you are my sister and I love you dearly, but you're nuts."

"I don't know what it means. He said—tell her to find the parallel lines."

Dianne's initial reaction—heightened irritation—evaporated. Parallel lines. A dream. A railroad track—but not a railroad track, not really.

It was uncanny.

Quickly, Nancy asked, "Dianne, what's wrong?"

Dianne's thoughts whirled like a kaleidoscope. Palmistry, astrology, fortunetelling—a Jack-of-all-trades circus performer, for heaven's sake. The man *had* to be phony. Besides, she was not even sure she believed such things were possible— even with someone sincere. Slowly, carefully, she looked at her sister. "Where is he—tonight?"

Startled, Nancy answered, "Huh?"

"Mark Hembric."

"Oh, Dianne, I *knew* he could help you! What does it mean —parallel lines?"

"I don't know," answered Dianne. "Maybe something to do with those charts Frank draws for his office. Look, wait here a sec. Give me the name and address. I want to go back to Dad's and call the baby sitter—let her know where I'll be."

It was almost eight-thirty when they arrived at the Vanorland apartment on Sutton Place. The apartment, Dianne decided, was downright intimidating in its opulent splendor. Next to this, even Frank's parents seemed poor. Society page wedding announcements flashed through her mind—Mr. and Mrs. So-and-so of Manhattan and Palm Beach announce—. This was the Manhattan apartment, complete with silk brocade furniture and skyline view, dominated by the United Nations building. Maybe a dozen folding chairs were set up in rows in the living room, supplementing three couches and two delicately peach pastel upholstered chairs. Dianne realized immediately that her clothes were inappropriate. Name designers dominated here.

A stunning girl of about twenty-two with auburn hair and the greenest eyes Dianne had ever seen stood in the foyer-to-living room entrance way, handing out three-by-five white file cards, envelopes and pencils. "Write a statement," she said. "Something personal. A fact known only to you. Then write your name on the outside of the envelope." A couple, apparently in their sixties, joined Dianne and Nancy. The girl included them in her continuing instructions. "Then place the card inside the envelope, seal the envelope and drop it in the box"—she pointed—"over there."

Dianne and Nancy took seats near the back of the room. "He's marvelous," said Nancy. "Dianne, he's absolutely marvelous."

"Where is he?"

Nancy did a quick survey, then settled back into her seat. "Not here yet. At least, I don't see him."

Beginning to feel slightly idiotic, Dianne looked at the ever-so-blank white card in her hand. Okay. Some fact known only to Dianne. Choose something to do with Frank. The last time she saw him. He went out for steak, then came back. *I'd rather have canned chili with you,* he said.

She glanced at Nancy. Had she told Nancy? No. Okay. She wrote, *Frank came back for chili.* Name on the outside of the envelope, card inside—seal the envelope. She left her seat, dropped the sealed envelope into the appropriately marked box, then returned to her place beside Nancy.

"What did you write?" asked Nancy.

Dianne smiled. "Nope."

First, Nancy looked startled. Then she laughed. "Cynic! You'll see."

It was about another ten minutes before everything seemed fully organized, all cards in the box and everyone seated. Dianne waited, somewhat hunched down in her chair. Like a circus, she thought, except that you're supposed to believe the elephants can fly. She glanced at the gold-trimmed velvet draperies. Expensive circus, she concluded.

"Look!" said Nancy. "That's Mark. He just came in."

Dianne, half turned in her seat, was startled. Mark Hembric walked up the aisle between the folding chairs. He was

younger than Dianne had expected—perhaps mid to late thir-
ties. He wore an almost cliché Madison Avenue gray suit
with a pale blue shirt and predominantly darker blue rep tie.
The effect was conventional—establishment, even down to the
white handkerchief in his pocket and highly shined black
loafers.

He was irritatingly handsome. Coal black hair lightly flecked
with gray, steel blue eyes. He was a young, rugged Laurence
Olivier in Marlboro Country on Sutton Place—brooding, magnetic, virile. Probably insufferably egotistical, Dianne decided,
perhaps resenting the dramatic effectiveness of his entrance.

He walked to a table at the front of the room and stepped
behind it, facing his audience. "Good evening," he said. His
voice was pleasant, subdued.

He began with something he called psychometry—information revealed through objects collected before his arrival from
various members of the audience. The first item was a locket.
He examined it, then closed his eyes, leaned one hand against
the table in front of him and held the locket in his fist, against
his forehead.

"I see—"

The room was silent.

"I see—an injury. A woman."

He opened his eyes—scanned the audience. Tentatively, a
woman across the aisle from Dianne raised her hand.

"It belonged to my mother," she said. Her face seemed
unnaturally pale.

"No," he answered quickly. "Do not give me any information. Let me find what the object tells me. I see—an older
woman."

Her voice barely more than a whisper, but still slicing

through the intense silence of the room, she answered, "She was sixty-eight."

"A woman no longer among us on this earth," he continued. "An accident. Freak accident. Sudden. Completely unexpected."

"Her car—" whispered the woman.

It was—hypnotic. Dianne continued to stare at him. Obviously, it was set up in advance, and yet—something about it—about *him*—eerie, magnetic, exciting, frightening!

He concluded the saga of the locket, then went through four more objects. By the end of the fourth, Dianne was convinced that the answer was *not* collusion.

About an hour later, he lifted the box containing the sealed envelopes and placed it on the table in front of him. He selected the first envelope, still sealed, and held it up to his head, eyes closed.

"I see the initials—J.L.," he said. "J—Joseph, John—no—Jim. Jim Lam—no, L-a-z—Lazen."

A man with gray hair, two rows ahead of Dianne, raised his hand.

"Mr. Lazen," said Mark Hembric. It was an announcement, not a question.

The man nodded.

"Mr. Lazen, you want to know—" Again, he closed his eyes, then continued, "You want to know what your granddaughter asked you to give her on her birthday. Your granddaughter asked for—" He smiled. "A horse she could keep in the kitchen."

Dianne could not see Jim Lazen's face, but she heard the startled intake of breath, saw him nod. Applause followed.

"Let's make sure we're right," said Mark. He opened the sealed envelope, removed the card and apparently read it, silently, then returned the nod. More applause, mingled with excited whispers. Mark tossed the envelope and card back into the box in front of him, then lifted the next envelope.

Same procedure—he held the envelope, still sealed, against his forehead and closed his eyes.

"I see the initials—D.K. D. Dierdre, Deborah—no. This is strange. I keep getting 'Ann,' but of course 'Ann' doesn't start with D. D-Ann. *Di*anne. Dianne K." His lips tightened, eyes still closed, envelope still pressed against his forehead. "K. Klear—Kleamen—no, Klaner? Yes. Dianne Klaner."

Dianne held her breath, feeling oddly naked. Nancy had told him she'd be there. D.K. Dianne Klaner. All he needed for that one was a reasonably good memory. Awkwardly, primarily because Nancy was prodding her, Dianne raised her hand.

He nodded. "And you, Mrs. Klaner, want to know—" Again, he closed his eyes.

I want to know what Frank came back for, she thought. I want you to tell me.

"You want to know—what Frank came back for." Blue eyes meeting hers with disconcerting, subtly arrogant self-assurance, he continued, "Frank came back for—food. Something to eat. Foreign food. Mexican. Yes. Frank came back for—chili."

Chapter Eight

The following morning, Wednesday, Amanda took Sarah to play with a neighbor's child, then returned to the house. After those two pointless encounters with Mr. Klaner the previous day—one during Sarah's nap when Amanda had taken him the peanut butter and jelly sandwich and another later that night, Amanda realized he might never admit his guilt. Therefore, the best thing to do was to kill him without further unnecessary delay. The strain—emotional and physical—of having him there was hardly worth a heart attack or heaven only knew what else might go wrong with a woman her age climbing all those stairs two or three times a day, worrying and thinking about him even when she wasn't climbing stairs.

Sarah out of the house, now, Amanda unlocked the door to the basement, flipped on the light which lighted the area by the washing machine, and went downstairs. Be well prepared. Rather like cooking, she thought. Her mother had firmly impressed on her the importance of having all ingredients and equipment laid out in advance. But not like cooking —not really. Now that she gave the comparison a second thought, she found it distasteful.

She walked directly to the old steamer trunk near the wringer washing machine. It had stood there through so many generations, accumulating—things—clothing, objects, but now it was almost empty. She first began emptying it when she first conceived her plan for Mr. Klaner. Not that she'd actually committed herself to going through with it at that time. Rather, working on the trunk was a way of reassuring herself that she *would* go through with it, even though she had continually suffered periods of anxiety during which her hands trembled so badly she could barely manage. But that was all past now.

No, it was not past. The palms of her hands were quite damp.

The trunk was black with ornate brass trimming and a medallion lock. It was about three and a half feet high—awkward, but manageable. She opened the lid, revealing now-faded rosebud wallpaper lining the sides and lid. Her view of the bottom was blocked by some very old draperies.

With the aid of a rusted step stool, she climbed into the trunk and removed the draperies. They were heavy—faded Burgundy-wine velvet, and her muscles ached from the weight of them.

Out of the trunk, now, she surveyed its empty interior. Yes, Mr. Klaner would fit in there. She'd have to double him up a bit. She shuddered. Her great grandfather had planned to keep his wife alive indefinitely. Under an assumed name, several weeks ago Amanda had rented an isolated summer cottage in Pennsylvania, near a lake. The lake was the intended final resting place for the trunk containing Mr. Klaner.

Amanda withdrew a check list from her apron pocket. The list was written on a sheet of note paper torn from a tablet she bought at the supermarket. Printed at the top were the words, "Things to Do Today," accompanied by assorted two-color sketches of various fruits and vegetables.

First on the list—empty trunk. She made a check mark.

Second—measure lumber. She had already measured the stairs. By covering the stairs with boards, she planned to create a ramp, not too steep if she began at the cage door and built height gradually. With Sarah's roller skates attached to a plank, she would tie the then-deceased Mr. Klaner to the plank and wheel him up the ramp. Unable to find her metal measurer, Amanda used a cloth tape measure. She Scotch-taped one end of it to the nearest piece of lumber and, pencil in hand, measured the board.

Approximately half an hour later, Amanda returned to the living room and sat on the couch. Still working on her list, she added "plastic dropcloth." No—*two* dropcloths. One to line the inside of the trunk, the other to wrap around Mr. Klaner. A bed sheet also. As far as she knew, all plastic dropcloths were transparent and she did not want to see him any more than necessary after he was dead. She wrote, "cut laundry markings from sheet."

Dead. Lord, it was ghastly. And yet she felt better than she had felt in a long time—steadier, perhaps partially because the whole procedure was becoming more mechanical to her. Shock, she decided, is a temporary emotion. When it wears off, we begin to deal with the problem in practical terms.

She glanced at the four clocks on the mantelpiece. It was approximately eleven o'clock. She was to pick up Sarah at noon. Note. Stop at hardware store on way home with Sarah and buy two plastic dropcloths.

She lifted the Manhattan Yellow Pages and flipped through. The profusion of display ads for moving companies was confusing—irritating. Marking that section with her finger, she closed the book.

What was the name of the company her neighbor who was caring for Sarah at that moment had used? So many young people had moved into that new building next door, but Amanda vaguely remembered this particular neighbor commenting that not one thing had been broken, nor had empty beer cans and cigarette butts been left all over the lobby. Now she remembered—North American Van Lines.

She looked it up.

"A trunk?" said the male voice on the other end of the line. "Well, yeah. We move trunks. Where's it going?"

"Rural delivery, about twenty miles outside of Burwick, Pennsylvania," answered Amanda. A summer cottage near a lake, she thought.

"Okay. Give me your name and address, tell me what's in the trunk—"

"What?"

"Name and address," he repeated. "We have to know where to pick it up."

"You asked me what's in it."

"Well, yeah. The insurance company wants to know."

With forced lightness, Amanda answered, "Oh, I don't want it insured. Really, it's not worth much."

"Well, then you'd want minimum insurance, but we do insure."

With greater effort, she maintained the lightness. "Goodness, do you *inspect* the contents?"

"Well, I don't know. They might."

Quickly, she hung up. It was all right, she reassured herself. She had not given her name. Still, she wondered whether her knees would have supported her had it been necessary to stand at that exact moment.

Patterns of sunlight on the floor had shifted considerably by the time Amanda next looked at the four clocks on the mantelpiece. It was approximately eleven forty-five—over half an hour since her call to North American Van Lines. And now—three calls later, she knew that not only North American Van Lines, but all of them might be just as likely to go peering and poking into that trunk.

Damn Mr. Klaner! Today was Wednesday. He had been in the cage approximately two days—since Monday night. The most nerve-shredding two days Amanda had ever experienced.

Well, she thought, memories of one of Sarah's storybooks echoing memories of Amanda's own childhood, *I, said the Little Red Hen.*

I'll do it myself.

Rent a truck. Hire someone to help her load it. She thought of the actresses who rented the upstairs apartment. She had seen them several times with boy friends—maybe the boy friends could use a few extra dollars. Or—if not, then perhaps some of the maintenance crew from that big new apartment building next door would be interested. A trunk. That was all. Just help her load a perfectly ordinary rather weathered steamer trunk onto a drive-it-yourself truck.

Hands unsteady, she again opened the Yellow Pages—found a truck rental service.

"But don't you have *anything* less expensive?" she asked, realizing in the same breath that she would have to pay it, whatever it cost.

"That's pretty much the standard rate, lady," said the man on the other end of the line. "Look, I don't understand. If it's just a trunk, why don't you call Railway Express?"

"Because the contents are—personal," she snapped. "Letters and papers and—things. Things nobody has any business inspecting."

"Inspecting? I don't understand."

"The insurance companies. They inspect, don't they?"

"Well, not Railway Express. At least not as far as I know. Not unless you want a *lot* of insurance."

"I don't want any!"

"Then call Railway Express."

Numbly, Amanda answered, "Thank you."

She called Railway Express.

Wednesday, 1:30 P.M. Dianne Klaner checked the file cabinets, desk and shelves in Frank's office. So far, no improper papers, letters, gift receipts—nothing she might object to having the police, a private detective or anyone else read. Relief mingled with renewed frustration. No evidence whatsoever of another woman—unless he had destroyed the evidence before leaving.

No. The other-woman theory still did not feel right. Especially now. Dianne sat at his desk, abstractedly fingering some of the pens and pencils in the top drawer. Some belonged to Frank, others bore the company name. She knew one particular pen belonged to Frank. It was a gold-filled Mark Cross ball point, which she had given him as a Christmas present two years ago. To the best of her knowledge, he used it constantly, leaving it at the office to avoid losing it. She slipped it into her purse.

Abruptly, she felt as though someone were staring at her. She glanced up, startled to see one of the programmers standing in the office doorway. His physical resemblance to Frank was remarkable. Dianne had seen him once before. Across a dimly lit room she had actually mistaken him for Frank. Ed Somethingorother. Ed and Frank were approximately the same age, same build, same coloring, very similar features. The resemblance, Dianne remembered, was purely physical.

"Excuse me," he said. Then, as now, his manner was intrusive, arrogant with swaggering pseudomasculinity. "I didn't realize you were still here, Mrs. Klaner," he continued. "I can come back later."

"Thank you," she answered, not caring if it inconvenienced him. "I'll be about another ten minutes."

Alone now, Dianne remembered the rest of the name. Ed Lucas. She saw him at an airport cocktail lounge table with Pete Marshall. Frank, Pete and Ed had just returned from a convention in California, and Dianne went to the airport to meet Frank. Ed's wife was also there, Dianne remembered— a tense overweight woman whose stiletto-sharp jealousy indicated valid foundation in Ed's past behavior. Strange that the memory remained clear. It happened years ago—at least four or five.

Wearily, Dianne stood up, took one last look at Frank's office. But not Frank's office, not really. The company's office. One of many, as Frank was one of many employees. A relatively small office, actually. Certainly his disappearance was inconvenient, but not earth-shaking. Business continued, almost as usual. For the first time, some of the things Frank had said to her so many times began to penetrate emotionally. You've got to reach for it, work for it—the carpeted office with the title on the door, because too many other guys want it. You've got to be good—better than they are. She thought of her father. Frank wanted so much more than her father had ever had or ever really wanted. Did Dianne also want more—the money *and* Frank's time? Perhaps she had been unfair to Frank. She knew it was not only the money Frank wanted. Without the challenge, the sense of accomplishment, the game, he would be unhappy no matter how much money he had. And yet, to feel that she was equally as important to him as the job—on a human level, more important—no, she decided, this was not an unreasonable need.

Abruptly fighting tears, she glanced at her watch. Almost two o'clock. Assuming she got a cab right away, there'd be no problem. Her appointment was at two-thirty.

Chapter Nine

"No," said Mark Hembric into the phone receiver, his voice firm. "Nothing circusy."

"*Circusy?* Have you any idea how many people watch Allan Burke?"

"I don't care. As far as I'm concerned, it's cheap sensationalism, and I don't want anything cheap. I've got a nice client practice. The kind of publicity you're talking about isn't going to help, and it could hurt. Come on, Hal. Get me Susskind —or the Today show."

"You don't just 'get Susskind,'" snapped Mark's new-found manager.

"Well try," returned Mark, his voice just as sharp. "What the hell am I paying you for?"

"So give me something to work with!" exploded Hal. "Every damn thing I come up with isn't good enough for you. So *you* come up with something, okay? Find the loot in a million-dollar bank robbery or jump in the river and save a kid nobody else knew was drowning. Something, *anything*—but get your name in the papers, and I don't mean the society columns for those Park Avenue mind-reading parties."

"Those parties," answered Mark evenly, "have helped establish a private clientele for me with fees ranging from twenty to sixty dollars per forty-five-minute session. Don't knock it. It pays the rent, very nicely."

"Mark—even Dunninger didn't start at the top."

"I'm prettier than Dunninger," answered Mark, dryly. "And I can match every damn trick Dunninger's got."

"Like hell you can."

Mark laughed. "Okay. It was an exaggeration. I could still give him some pretty stiff competition for a TV audience."

"Mark—Dunninger has a *name*."

"Okay, okay."

"So *do* something. Get your name in the papers. Think up something."

"Yeah, but—look, Hal, we're not together on this. I know it takes longer my way, but I'm preserving an image. Dignity, honesty, unpretentiousness. Humor, because you've got to ride with the heckling, but you can still get the publicity. You don't have to turn carnival. I want converts, Hal—not just the preestablished fanatics. I want everybody who follows Dixon, Holzer, Woodruf, Leek, Dunninger—*plus*. That's where the image comes in. That's why it's worth it, even if it takes longer."

The downstairs buzzer sounded.

"I've got to go," said Mark. "A client. Look, maybe we can hash this out over lunch sometime next week. I'll call you."

"Okay. Mark, maybe I do see what you mean. But you've still got to give me something to work with."

"Okay. I'll see if I can think of anything." He hung up. Hal was probably right. Mark needed publicity, but—the Allan Burke show? No. He did not need publicity that badly this quickly.

He pushed the buzzer to release the downstairs door, and glanced at his watch. Two thirty-five. Five minutes late. This was the blonde with the missing husband, Dianne Klaner. Mark took one last quick survey of the apartment. Dark blue draperies pulled back just far enough to permit the right amount of soft sunlight to enter through the off-white curtains beyond. The rug was blue tweed, the furniture predominantly brown. The building was new, and the apartment aura was modern. Part of his image. No cobwebs, no spooks. He wore gray slacks, a blue sport shirt, gray tweed jacket and highly shined loafers.

He double-checked his notes. Dianne Klaner. Twenty-dollar fee. Nancy Meyer's sister. Born in Delaware. Moved to New York when her father's company transferred him, about fifteen years ago. Nice break, Dianne being Nancy's sister. Occasionally, Nancy had even talked about Dianne's husband.

He remembered Dianne exceptionally well. Something about her eyes and general coloring reminded him of his ex-wife. He'd been twenty-one, then—a carnival escape artist in a pitched tent in Ohio. The girl he married was nineteen, a dogmatically virginal receptionist in a local dentist's office. The marriage lasted not quite two years. Funny—he still thought of her sometimes, but the feelings which accompanied the thoughts were vague. He was thirty-five, now. The marriage might have been a lifetime ago.

The apartment doorbell rang.

He closed his notebook, returned it to the desk drawer, then locked the drawer and slipped the key into his pocket. Disposing of a piece of lint on his jacket sleeve, he opened the door. "Come in," he said, stepping back.

Dianne sat on the couch and nervously fished out a cigarette. The apartment was not what she had expected. It was too—clean. Chic, in a quiet, masculine way. "Aren't you supposed to have a crystal ball and a towel over your head?" she asked.

He laughed. "Well, I try not to be cliché about it. I suppose

I could post some horoscope charts on the wall if you want me to."

In spite of the fact that she neither liked nor trusted him, she smiled. "Have you really got horoscope charts?"

"Sure. Give me your birth date."

"I'm impressed. Astrology, palmistry, telepathy—that's quite a line-up. How's your batting average?"

Eyes never leaving hers, he seated himself in a chair opposite the couch where Dianne sat. "So-so," he answered.

"That's not very impressive."

"Is that why you came here? To be impressed?"

"No. I came here to see whether you could help me find my husband, but before we get into it, I'd like to know a little more about you. Are you honest, Mr. Hembric?"

Carefully, he answered, "About as honest as the next guy, I suppose."

"That's evasive. Who is 'the next guy'?"

"Okay. You. I'm as honest as you are, Mrs. Klaner."

She felt her face flush, slightly. "What's that supposed to mean?"

"Means your feelings are mixed on whether you even want your husband back."

The color in her face deepened, this time motivated by anger. "Nancy told you that. How *dare* she!"

"You told me that yourself," he answered irritably. "You project it. There are a lot of things about you—about anyone. An aura. The nebulousness of your feelings towards your husband are part of you, at this moment."

Awkwardly, she answered, "What else?"

"Money. You're scared. You know you may have to get a job, but you also know you'll have one hell of a time finding somebody to look after the kids."

Disconcerted, she answered, "Go on."

"Your kids are driving you nuts, and you're worried about your feelings towards them. You know they're upset—they pick it up from you, even though you've told them your husband's out of town on a business trip. You're afraid that now that they especially need you emotionally, you're shortchanging them."

"How did you know what Frank came back for?"

"You knew. I picked it out of your mind."

"What if I'd lied—concentrated on something that wasn't true? Would it have thrown you?"

"I don't know. No matter what you concentrated on, part of you still knew the right answer. I might have tuned in on that part."

"What am I thinking right now?"

"I haven't the faintest idea."

"Why not?"

"Because it doesn't work that way. ESP is not some little monkey that'll hop when you say hop. I spent hours yesterday afternoon tuning in on that group. It's like—I don't know—radio waves. You tune in—when you can. Sometimes it comes in loud and clear, sometimes it's only signals and sometimes it's a complete washout."

"Then what am I paying you for?"

"You're paying me to try."

Her voice cracked. "Can you tell me whether he's alive?"

"Maybe. I don't know. Did you bring what I asked you to bring?"

"An object that belongs to him," repeated Dianne, remembering Mark's words the night of the party. "Something he used regularly, preferably metal because metal retains vibra-

tions exceptionally well. Yes," she answered, opening her purse.
"I brought a ball point pen."

The phone rang.

Mark's immediate reaction was irritation. "Sorry," he said.
"I should have taken it off the hook." He crossed to the desk,
lifted the receiver. "Hello?"

Dianne lit another cigarette. Something was wrong—about
him. What?

"Well, I'm busy right now," he said. "I'll call you back,
okay?"

There was something in the tone of his voice—a woman,
Dianne decided. He was talking to a woman, and she was
not a client.

"I'm with a client," he said into the receiver. Dianne remembered his previous statements on aura. The aura surrounding Mark at that moment was irritation mixed with
caution. He wanted to get rid of his caller, but also wanted
to avoid offending her. "I'll call you back as soon as I can,"
he repeated. Then, more gently, but awkwardly, "You know
I do."

You know I do—what, Dianne wondered. Love you? Good
grief, the guy had girl friend trouble.

"Yes," said Mark into the receiver. "I will." He broke the
connection, then laid the receiver beside the hook. "Sorry,"
he repeated to Dianne.

"It's all right," she answered. He returned to his chair,
and Dianne handed him the ball point pen—but not Frank's
pen. This one, she had purchased in a stationery store on
her way to Mark's apartment.

"Just tell me he's alive," said Dianne, fear mingling with
hope. Let him hand the pen back to her, tell her the "vibrations" were off that day.

Gently, he answered, "I can't tell you whether he's alive. At least not right away. The last time he used this pen, there may have been something he felt very strongly about. If so, the pen might contain powerful vibrations, even if—" Deliberately, he left the sentence unfinished. "Its primary value now," he went on, "is to help open the passageways for psychic contact."

He leaned forward in the chair, eyes closed, elbows on his knees, hands clenched against his forehead. In his hands, he held the stationery store pen.

Tell him, Dianne thought. He'll find out and be angry. Yet the feeling persisted—something wrong about Mark Hembric. Confused, Dianne waited—watched his trancelike concentration. Obviously, he did not know that pen had never belonged to Frank. It was an act! Except—how the dickens had he known Frank came back for chili?

Mark's body seemed to go limp. Then, abruptly, he sat back in the chair, hands on the arms. He looked tired—as though he had just been through a physically draining ordeal. Oh, he was good at it, he was lovely. Dianne braced herself for some scrap of personal information Nancy had probably given him.

He let out a deep breath. "I'm sorry," he said. "I'm not getting anything. I may have picked up a little, but I think I picked it up from you, rather than the pen. He was very much in your thoughts. But this"—he held out the pen and shook his head—"nothing. I'm sorry."

Dianne's face grew scarlet. She felt like a grade school child caught copying answers on a test. "All right," she said. "It never belonged to him. I bought it in the stationery store across the street, right after I got out of the cab."

"Well, congratulations. The forty-five minutes are up, and

we're nowhere. That'll be twenty dollars, please. Do you want to pay now, or shall I bill you?"

"Stop it," she snapped right back at him. "I wanted to be sure—"

"You'll never be sure. There is no such thing in this business."

"Do you have someone else coming? Now, I mean."

He hesitated, then sat back. "No. Did you bring anything that really belongs to him?"

"Yes. A ball point pen."

A slightly sardonic look touched his eyes. "Give it to me."

She gave him the pen which really belonged to Frank. Mark took the first pen she had given him and tossed it to her. She picked it up from the couch beside her and toyed with it, uncomfortably.

Same procedure—he leaned forward, eyes closed, pen clenched in his fists against his forehead.

Contact Frank, Dianne thought. And what if Frank did not want to be contacted? She closed her eyes. Another woman? No—please, no.

His voice barely more than a whisper, Mark said, "I see—"

Dianne waited, hardly daring to breathe.

"Wait a sec—" said Mark, "I—I'm getting something. He— it's something to do with where he is—or was, shortly after he went out that last night you saw him. He—it's something to do with parallel lines."

Dianne stared at him. He seemed unreal—as though magic had materialized him and might dematerialize him just as abruptly. Parallel lines. "But what does it mean," she whispered.

Quickly, with his hand, Mark motioned for her to be silent.

"He's—unhappy," Mark continued. "Upset. Tremendous emotional upheaval."

"He's alive!" answered Dianne, no longer able to control the surge of emotion which begged for release through tears.

"I don't know," answered Mark. "I can't quite place it in time. It's recent. Dark. Surrounded by darkness."

"Where?"

"Near. Somewhere in New York City. But—" Almost as though he were speaking through pain, he continued, "But I can't get the time. You're very much in his mind."

"Frank—" she whispered, lips trembling. Mark no longer seemed mortal, his voice no longer emanating from a human body. He was time itself and man's faith through all time that such things were possible. "Help me," she continued. "Please—"

His body grew limp. He sat back, stretched out in the chair, as though exhausted. His eyes were still closed, but there was no longer anything otherworldly about him. He opened his eyes—looked at Dianne. Voice sharp, he said, "Get yourself a private detective."

Chapter Ten

Kathy Gillmore checked her watch. Another ten minutes and she could wash the Clairol black goop from her roots, re-emerging completely auburn-haired. The main problem was, what if Mark returned her call while she was running water in the bathroom? Tentatively, she lifted the telegram from the coffee table. A running part in a TV series which she had auditioned for several months ago was now open to her, but they were filming in California.

The phone rang.

She jumped, then grabbed it. "Hello?"

"Kathy. Hi."

Not Mark—Jeanne, one of Kathy's roommates. "Oh, hi," said Kathy. "I thought you were Mark. I called him—he said he'd call me back."

"You mean you wasted the cost of a phone call?" asked Jeanne. "Why didn't you just sit and concentrate?"

"Very funny," answered Kathy dryly.

"When are you going to tell me how he does that mind reading trick?"

"Never. He made me sign a paper before he told me."

"You stand at the door as the people come in, and you tell them—"

"Jeanne, will you please say what you want and get off the phone?"

"Okay. I'm sorry. I wondered how it came out—the marry-me-or-off-I-go-to-California bit."

"I haven't said it yet," answered Kathy awkwardly. "That's not the kind of thing you say over the phone. I want to see him."

"Well, when you do—honey, remember all those chains and locks he picked his way out of in the carnival before he got into the mind reading bit. I mean, from what you said, he's quite an escape artist—"

"Jeanne, please, don't." Her voice cracked. "I'm not a lock or a chain. I love him."

"Look, remember me? I'm your bridesmaid. It's just—if you do find you want a soft shoulder—I really do have to go to Larry's party tonight, but if you want me, call me and I'll come home."

"Thank you," whispered Kathy. Slowly, she replaced the receiver.

Tears flooded her eyes. Who was she trying to kid? Mark would not marry her. She knew it and so did Jeanne. Sleep with her—sure, why not? Well, no, that wasn't exactly true. If one of them had seduced the other, it was she who had seduced Mark. Mark was far too intelligent to court this kind of involvement with a girl who knew how he did his tricks.

She washed her hair, then returned to the living room, a towel draped over her shoulders.

She glanced at the phone, then walked to the window. At least the building walls were thick enough to keep out the summer heat and mugginess, unless the day was unbearable. She parted the curtain—that ridiculous not-too-clean flowered curtain, and looked down onto 91st Street. From her window on the second floor, she saw the tops of the stone lions which guarded the entrance way to the building, although the orange door she had passed through countless times was beyond her line of vision.

What was she looking for? Mark?

Angrily, she let the curtain fall back into place. Maybe— if she threatened him—she could be an awfully good wife to him, after they were married.

The room, abruptly, seemed oppressive. Mrs. Hilton had "decorated" it herself—with swirls and curls and flowers all over the place. The rug was a tragedy, as though designed to dispose of vermin through pure terror. At least the condition of the walls was adequate, for an old building, but the color was seasick green. The red phone was Jeanne's contribution —let's liven this place up, quoth Jeanne, after Mrs. Hilton had indignantly refused them permission to redecorate.

Kathy shuddered, then walked to the ornately carved mahogany sideboard and switched on her transistor radio. Admit radio sounds to the room like a guest—anything beyond the deafening silence of an unringing telephone.

News. Vietnam.

She switched to another station. Herb Alpert and the Tijuana Brass. Great! Mark had a passion for FM radios, forever tuning in on something classical. Kathy suspected his motivation was partially snobbery—aiming for a cultural background his now-dead Chicago-slum mother and father had never had.

The music ended, the news came on. Kathy stood by the window and dried her hair, not really listening. City official accused of taking bribes. Some kind of a strike. Strikes all over the place in New York. Was it that bad in California? This strike was wildcat, strictly local. New York City Railway Express on strike. Then—taxi strike threatened. *Taxi?*

Abruptly irritated by the sound of a voice rather than music, Kathy Gillmore switched to another station.

Stunned, Dianne Klaner sat on the couch and stared at Mark Hembric. "A private detective?" she repeated.

"Yes." Then, more gently, he continued, "I told you, I can't place it in time. But—danger. I get a clear sense of danger."

"Yes," whispered Dianne. "I've felt it too."

As though she had not spoken, Mark continued, "Danger, urgency. Look, sometimes—occasionally, I get a clear picture, but other times—only snatches—signals. And that's all I'm getting here. Sure, it may improve—but what if it doesn't? Play it safe, Dianne. As safe as possible. Get yourself a private detective."

Numbly, she answered, "Money—and the kids."

"Huh?"

"My father offered to help, but he can't really afford it. And Frank's parents aren't well. Besides, as soon as a private detective started asking questions all over the place, the kids would know something was wrong. And—well, frankly, I'm afraid to get a detective. It would feel so final. This way, I suppose I'm better able to keep kidding myself that Frank's liable to walk in the door any minute."

"You came to me for help and advice. The best I can offer you of both is, hire a private detective."

Slowly, very slowly, Dianne answered, "All right." She thought of her money—hers and Frank's. Not much, really, but enough to start with. A few thousand plus some stock. And with Frank simply missing like this, there'd be no insurance money. Before she married Frank, she had been a secretary. Brush up her skills, go back. She would have to pay someone to care for the children. She remembered how much trouble she had had trying to find someone even to clean for a day or two each week. The rates for domestic help were astronomical. Could she earn enough to pay eighty or ninety dollars a week—which was a low estimate for even competent domestic help, plus meet her basic living expenses? Dear Lord, even if she moved from their present apartment into the cheapest slum in New York and virtually gave up food, she still could not make it.

Nancy? No, Nancy would go raving nuts with four small children. Frank's parents? Ridiculous. Although they tried to be kind to Dianne, they had never felt she was quite good enough for Frank. If Dianne were financially dependent on them, they would virtually own her—and the children. She thought of her father. Start all over again, at his age, supporting and caring for a family with small children? Foster home? Her reaction bordered on pain. Never! Day nursery, semi-supported by welfare?

"Well, I guess that's it," said Mark.

"Not quite," answered Dianne. "When will I see you again, what can you do in the meantime and is there anything I can do—psychically? Parallel lines. Nancy said you told her to tell me to find the parallel lines, but I don't understand. I can't make any sense out of it."

"Parallel lines are the only thing I can place in time," he answered, not really looking at her. "Wherever he is—right now, he's close enough to reach out and touch them. If we knew what they represent and where they are, we'd know where your husband is. But we don't know."

"Maybe—a chart. He's always looking at charts and diagrams. They're part of his work."

"No." He sounded definite. "These are not part of a drawing. They're descriptive of a three-dimensional thing. A thing you could touch with your hands."

"But what can I *do*," she asked. "Dreams—feelings. I feel so helpless, confused."

"Dreams," he answered, almost sharply. "If you dream something you feel strongly about, write it down. There may be a clue in it. Get a collection of clues, maybe you'll find a pattern. Also—impulse. Instinct. Follow it."

She smiled. "If I followed instinct, I'd have walked out of here quite some time ago."

Startled, he answered, "Oh?"

"No, please don't be offended. It's a mixed feeling—instinct —whatever you'd call it. It says that what you've done here today isn't real—isn't what it seems to be even though I know it couldn't be anything else. But that same instinct says—" She broke off, then continued, "Isn't this ridiculous? It says I'm closer to finding Frank now than I would be if I hadn't come."

He made no comment.

Abruptly, she stood up. "What do I owe you? A fortune."

"You owe me twenty bucks."

She hesitated. He charged for his time. She owed him more. Then, "All right. Thank you. Really, thank you very much."

He rose to his feet and took the money.

Dianne wanted to help him. Help him out of the mood he seemed to have fallen into trying to help her, and yet she knew she could not. She did not know him—love him—all the things someone who's unhappy reaches out for. Also— or perhaps even more important, he did not want her to know him. She felt it with absolute sureness. His feelings, in her presence, were locked up tight and that was the way he wanted it. All right. Respect it. Respect him.

"When will I see you again?" she asked.

"Leave it open," he answered. "If I feel I have anything worth anything, I'll call you."

It startled her. Don't call us, we'll call you? "All right," she said, with no intentions of letting it drop.

He walked to the door with her and seemed preoccupied with other thoughts even before she left.

Holding the twenty dollars in his hand, he returned to the chair where he had sat facing Dianne. Well, hell, money was money.

No, this was *her* money, and she had damned little of it with two kids to support and hubby off to nowheresville. Mark's mother had supported two kids—Mark and a brother, six years younger, both born without benefit of clergy and both with different fathers. Strange—they were all dead now. No, maybe not. Maybe his brother's father was still alive—somewhere. The main thing Mark remembered about him—aside from the fact that they'd liked each other, was that he had taken Mark to his first carnival.

Mark pocketed the twenty dollars, then glanced at his watch. Ten minutes to four. Next client due at four o'clock.

Something he was supposed to do—what? He glanced at the phone receiver, still off the hook. No wonder he had not thought of it right away. Kathy Gillmore. Hell hath no fury and all that crap. She knew too much about him. Not too much for a business partner, but far too much for a scorned bed partner. He walked to the desk and called her.

"Hi, Mark." The cheerful tone sounded forced, put him on guard. "I'm sorry I bothered you when you were with a client," she continued.

"It's okay, honey, but in the future, if I tell you I'm with somebody, just drop the conversation, all right?"

"Okay."

She was too young for him—one of the main reasons why he had selected her for his act. Lovely to look at but too young for him to end up in bed with her. He knew when he hired her that she had a crush on him, but that was how he had thought of it—a crush. Something teen-agey. Yet after that first night—any time he wanted it, any way he wanted it—he was hooked. Hell, maybe he was still hooked, but not that hooked.

"Mark," she went on, "I want to see you."

Something in her voice increased his suspicions. Some brand-new approach to a lifetime of marital bliss? His whole relationship with her had become akin to walking on egg-shells. "Well, I'm pretty jammed up here," he said. "Could we make it sometime next week?"

Pause. Then, blurting it out over the phone, she answered, "I won't be here next week. That's what I wanted to tell you. I'm leaving for California—tonight or tomorrow. I have a running part in a TV series being filmed out there."

It stunned him. He was used to her. No, more than that, he—liked her. Now that he was off the hook, relief mingled with a peculiar sense of emptiness.

"Mark?"

"Yeah, I'm still here."

"Well, say something!"

"I'm sorry. Takes a minute to soak in. I'd like to see you, before you go."

Breathlessly, she answered, "Mark, I won't go. Not if you don't want me to."

The eggshells were back, surrounding him. "Of course I don't want you to—but it sounds like a good opportunity for you to be seen, Kathy. Who knows what it might lead to?

And who knows when—if ever, you might get another break like this?"

"Mark, I don't care. I don't want the part. I want you!"

"Kathy"—his mouth felt unnaturally dry—"I want you to take it."

Pause.

A sharp click, followed by the silence of a broken connection.

Slowly, Mark replaced the receiver, the palm of his hand leaving a sweat smear on it.

Chapter Eleven

Numbly, Frank Klaner leaned back on the now-familiar pile of rags. Time no longer had meaning. It was a world without color or form, without sound except for whatever sound he made in conjunction with the mysterious continuing hum. Like a giant bee gone berserk eternally hovering at exactly the same pitch. He reminded himself that he was not dead, caught in some surrealistic limbo of unbroken, droning, black, black time. His life prior to being here seemed some distant fantasy. Was Dianne real? A woman. His wife. She seemed real. So much a part of him, so completely in his thoughts. At times, it seemed unimportant that thoughts were all he had now. The thoughts—and feelings evoked by the thoughts were so real. Could any reality be more intense? Here, there were no distractions except of course for those timeless, sporadic visits by the Old Woman. He knew she was not really "old," but in his mind, she kept changing. A hag. A Walt Disney classical witch, then a sweet little grandmother, then one of the key punch supervisors from his office. *Office* had become a buzz word within his thoughts. Dianne was constant, but the office was a whirling kaleidoscope. He had to grab the office, hold it still, get a perspective on it. For Dianne and the kids, time had stopped, but the office continued to function, slicing through the almost self-hypnotic peace of random thoughts wandering through the surrounding blackness. The office would not wait.

Wait for what?

Wait for him to Get Out. And yet there was no way he could Get Out—not without the old woman's help.

There was an old woman who lived in a shoe.

With a cage in the toe, he added, searching for a next line.

He tried to stop his thoughts, but they flooded in on him. Could his mind seriously deteriorate this quickly?

No. His mind was okay because he still knew who he was, where he was and was very much aware of the fact that on occasion, his thoughts seemed to slip. As long as he retained logical awareness, he decided, he would be all right.

Fantasies closed in on him—often sexual, almost equally as often relative to success in his work. He ran his hand over the beard on his face. Even more than he wanted a shave and a bath, he wanted a cigarette. Food too. How long since her last visit?

He knew she planned to kill him, and there were times when the thought amused him. No one could kill him, least of all that *New Yorker* cartoon matron. The beat of his heart was too real, he was too sensually aware of everything around him. He smelled the faint odor of rust which had clung to his hands and clothing ever since he tried to dislodge the leg iron chain from its wall socket. He tasted salt on his lips. Sweat. His body had been covered with it ever since he first regained consciousness in the cage.

Stiffly, he rolled onto his side, closed his eyes. Then—no. The escapist sleep he sought was far too close to Frank's concept of death—an end to all consciousness, even consciousness of blackness.

He opened his eyes and saw light. A small rectangle of

light pouring in onto the floor outside his cell. The old woman, grandmother, key-punch supervisor was about to visit him.

He pulled himself up onto his elbows, faced the front of the cage. Certainly it was not the first time she had come, yet this time he was intensely afraid. For an instant, he wanted to kill her—slowly, with his hands. Quietly, softly, his emotions went numb. Hate was gone. Fear remained, but quietly now. A steady background pitch of fear which made his hands damp, his mouth dry and his heart beat a little too quickly, but that was all.

The squeaking door. Like a Halloween satire. Trick or treat. What do you want, Old Woman? What treat? What in hell do you want from me?

Amanda Hilton entered the area of the cage, carrying a lantern and flashlight, both lit. She was upset. Railway Express was on strike. She dared not leave his remains inside the trunk in her basement indefinitely. Aside from the fact that the gas man or anyone else with business in the basement might notice a no-doubt increasingly distasteful odor, even with Airwick, Amanda knew that her own nerves would not do well under the strain of knowing she had a—the thought was too repugnant. A *corpse* in her basement.

She would have to wait until the instant the strike was settled. It was a strictly local wildcat strike—might be settled any day, any minute.

She beamed her flashlight into the cell, then pushed a paper bag containing food through the bars, away from where he might be able to reach her.

"Thanks," he offered dryly, not moving. He was ravenous, but damned if he'd let her know it.

"You should pray, Mr. Klaner. Pray for God to take your soul."

An icy chill ran through him. "Will you pray for me, Mrs. Hilton?" he asked with tight-lipped irony.

Startled, she hesitated. Then, "I don't know. Perhaps—someday."

"I'd like to remember Miriam. I met lots of girls in California. Lots of girls in many states."

For the first time, Amanda wondered—could Miriam have given him a false name? She flipped off the flashlight, stood there in the soft pale glow of the lantern. Quietly, she answered, "Miriam was a computer programmer. A plain-looking girl, but a good girl. Thirty years old and no man had ever improperly touched her. A nice girl, Mr. Klaner, until she went to that convention in California and met you. In that one night with you, Mr. Klaner, she became pregnant."

Stunned, Frank sat up. *"Pregnant? By me?"*

"Don't you dare pretend you didn't know," spat Amanda, trembling now. "She called you—even met you outside your office. First you said you'd deny even knowing her, then you offered to help her get an abortion. She liked to draw, Mr. Klaner. She drew pictures of you—constantly. Good pictures. Even if you hadn't given her your right name, I'd have recognized you from the pictures."

Frank closed his eyes, took his time. "Mrs. Hilton—granted, there are probably many things in my life which I have forgotten. But no man could forget whether he had ever been unfaithful to his wife—which I haven't—nor could he forget a girl who came to his office and accused him of fathering her unborn child."

"You still deny it." Frustration mingled with philosophical acceptance. "Sarah is your daughter," Amanda continued.

THERE WAS AN OLD WOMAN

"Sarah?" answered Frank, more confused.

"My granddaughter. You saw her—she came out of her room, and you saw her. She said you smiled at her. Smiled at her, indeed! You tried to kill her, before she was born."

Even though Frank knew she could not release him even if he did convince her, he answered, "I don't suppose you'd let me talk to Miriam—"

Amanda drew herself up to her full height and fought unsuccessfully to keep her voice steady and dignified. "Miriam is dead. Six weeks after Sarah was born, Miriam committed suicide."

At a loss for words, Frank answered, "I'm sorry, but—"

"Sorry? Seems it should mean more to you than that. I don't know why," she continued, almost as though speaking to herself. "Perhaps because it means so much to me. And Sarah. Sarah asks about her parents sometimes. Oh, not that she remembers Miriam—it's just that she's noticed the other children have mothers to take care of them, not grandmothers all the time."

"Mrs. Hilton, I—" He broke off, helplessly. What could he say that he had not already said?

Disconcerted, Amanda switched on the flashlight and walked, quickly, to the exit door. She felt embarrassed—to go on and on like that about Miriam in front of a man who did not care, had never cared. The door squeaked open, then squeaked and clanged shut, somewhere beyond the range of Frank's vision. Amanda had forgotten the lantern. Still lit, it remained on the floor opposite the cage.

Quickly, Frank went for the food she had brought. For the first time, in the dim glow of the lantern, he read the letters on the soda can. Diet Pepsi-Cola. Hell, it was funny. The sandwich, as usual, was peanut butter and jelly.

Both rested uneasily on his stomach. For one split second he thought—then, no. She could not put anything into a peel-top soda can without disturbing the seal, and Frank was sure the seal had been intact. As for the sandwich—even she would not come up with a poison peanut butter and jelly sandwich. When the time came, she would probably make a menu change. Something subtle, he thought dryly, like curry or chili.

Odd—chili stuck in his mind. Something to do with Dianne. He remembered now. The last time he saw her, they were going to have chili together. Then—the call, his brief case.

To hell with the brief case, he wanted his wife. Couldn't he spend more time with her? He not only loved her, he liked her—liked being with her. Maybe on some of the nights when he had to work late, she could meet him for dinner. Was a vacation really unthinkable? Maybe part of the problem was ineffective delegation of responsibility. Reorganize—free more of his own time.

Tears stung his eyes—a nerve reaction. Play it out. Loosen up. He wanted his kids. It had never before seriously occurred to him that they might grow up without him.

How *dare* that maniac keep him locked up down here!

California? Miriam Hilton? He lay down, his muscles aching with tension. He started to shake. Then—slowly, gradually— he was all right now. Gratefully, he glanced at the lantern. No more wandering fantasies, no more borderline confusion between what was real and what was imagined.

With his face toward the lantern, he watched the slightly flickering light.

Amanda Hilton reached her kitchen and, breathlessly, sat on the nearest chair. The climb—all of it, was too much for her. Her heart beat painfully fast, throbbing through her temples and her body was covered with a thin film of perspiration.

She glanced at the chipped, gilded kitchen clock. Eight-twenty. Far too early to go to bed, although she was exhausted. The floor should be mopped and most of the dinner dishes were still stacked in the sink, unwashed. Perhaps Miriam had been right in wanting to buy a dishwasher, although certainly she should have consulted Amanda before permitting them to install that special outlet next to the cellar entrance way. Christmas present, indeed! Now, with no appliance plugged into it, the outlet was a constant source of worry to Amanda. A refrigerator repairman had given Amanda quite a lecture on basic principles of electricity when he caught Sarah playing nearby with a hairpin. She could have been killed, he explained. So many ways a child might be killed. People usually tended to think of cars and street accidents, but most accidents—Amanda had read, take place in the home.

Angrily, Amanda stood up. This whole mood was Mr. Klaner's fault, she decided. He made it seem real that anyone could die. Even Sarah—or Amanda.

She started to wash the dishes. The feel of the soap suds was familiar, even pleasant.

A new fear—or rebirth of an old fear, took hold. What if, even with the ramp, she was unable to move the deceased Mr. Klaner into the trunk?

She tried to reassure herself. She had gotten him down—she could get him up. And yet she realized the two directions were quite different.

Scratching abstractedly at some dried spaghetti sauce on a plate, Amanda recognized a new possibility. Mr. Klaner could *walk* to the trunk. She could—knock him out with sleeping pills in his food, go into the cage and remove the leg iron. Chain his hands behind him, chain both ankles with just enough slack for him to walk. Gag him. When he regained consciousness—a poker might do—prod him to walk to the trunk, *then* kill him.

Eight-thirty. WPAT carried news on the half hour. She wiped her hands on a greasy flowered dish towel, then reached for the vacuum-tube radio on top of her time-yellowed refrigerator. Quickly, she withdrew her hand—a cockroach!

She grabbed a magazine to swat it, but by the time she turned around again, the roach was gone. She shuddered. They weren't *too* bad to look at, but she constantly dreaded the possibility of one someday actually crawling onto her. It might be nice to move away from this house, away from the bugs. The bugs seemed almost a part of the very plaster which covered the walls. Generations of cockroaches following the generations of Amanda's family, except that the roaches seemed to have grown bigger and stronger, while Amanda's family—she broke off. Only herself and Sarah now.

Carefully, she turned on the radio, then returned to the sink. Plane crash. Amanda added the last dish—Sarah's ice-cream dish—to those already in the sink. City official accused of taking bribes. She added a little more hot water. Quintuplets born at New York Hospital. My goodness, quintuplets! Railway Express. Amanda paused, shut off the water and listened.

Railway Express was still on strike.

Chapter Twelve

Dreams. Images. Fading. Parallel lines. Stripes. Bars. A fence. Picket fence. An orange picket fence, fading into the distance. The whole world seemed washed in orange. An orange zoo, orange tigers and lions.

"Mommy. *Mommy—*"

Dianne Klaner opened her eyes. Sunlight, sharp and stinging. Jimmy was perched on the bed beside her. Still not quite awake, she reached out and hugged him. He settled down beside her, momentarily content, quiet.

"Mother—" Tracy, this time. Dianne turned her head, slightly. To Tracy, she was "mother," usually with an unnecessarily strong accent on the second syllable. "Mommy" was for babies, like Jimmy. Proud of her new-found kindergarten-taught ability to tell time, Tracy continued in the same precociously authoritative tone, "Mother, it's eight o'clock."

Dianne hesitated—basked in a few remaining seconds of relaxed physical comfort. Abruptly, she sat up. "Okay," she said, "let's get dressed right away. No poking around. Then there'll be plenty of time to eat your orange juice."

Tracy giggled. "You said, 'eat your orange juice.'"

"I said, 'eat your *breakfast*,'" answered Dianne lightly. "Go on—scoot."

Alone now, she got out of bed, grabbed her robe. Vague

memories of a dream still lingered. Darnit. Gone—completely. Oh, Lord, Mark told her to keep a record. What was the dream?

She dressed the kids, prepared breakfast, then dressed herself—brown tweed skirt and dark green overblouse.

She left Tracy at school, then changed her route home, to avoid other mothers she knew. Although she knew logically that it was ridiculous, she continued to feel that Frank's disappearance was her fault. Something was terribly wrong about her. If she got too close to other people, they would sense it, see it. They would be angry or disgusted with her, and rightfully so.

"Where are we goin'?" asked Jimmy.

"Hum? Oh. Nowhere special."

Intrigued by the new route home, he broke free of her hand and ran ahead of her. Instinctively, she started after him, then changed her mind. Let him run. Wouldn't it be lovely if she, like Jimmy, could cut loose and run!

She wanted to cry. It was a beautiful day. The odor, freshness and pale green of spring was still evident, now accented by the deeper, richer green of early summer. Early summer in the city. Trees sprouted from concrete sidewalks. Landscaped apartment building lawns and window boxes brightened up after the winter brown-black of last year's dead flowers. People without coats. Chic people in this neighborhood. Chic, like Frank's parents. Dianne would probably receive a letter from them in a day or so—one of those I-know-you're-busy-but-why-haven't-you-written jabs at Frank.

She planned to call Nancy's husband that night. Bill was a lawyer—primarily corporate law, but still the best lead Dianne had on finding a reputable private detective. She now regretted not having hired one sooner.

Jimmy ran back to her and grabbed her hand. He stopped—looked up at her. "Don't cry, Mommy," he said.

How simple it was to Jimmy. Don't cry, that's all. "I'll try not to, darling," she said.

They continued to walk, hand in hand now. Abruptly, Dianne realized they had gone too far, East 89th Street.

Still holding Jimmy's hand, she signaled for a cab. Why not? Cut loose and run. The apartment, with Frank so much a part of it, had become oppressive to Dianne. A cab stopped and she opened the door. "Go on, Jimmy. Scoot over." He scrambled to the far side of the seat and Dianne followed, but gracefully.

"Where to?" asked the driver.

"Through the park," she said. She had nineteen dollars in her wallet. The day was beautiful. Cut loose and run—for ten or fifteen minutes, perhaps. Then—home. The apartment.

The driver took the nearest park entrance—96th Street. The floor of the cab was littered with cigarette butts and general refuse. An ad for a credit card service was stuck onto the back of the driver's seat, with the words TAKE ONE over a pocket marked Application Blank, but there was nothing left to take. She thought of Frank—cigarettes and credit cards. A plastic shield separated the driver from his passengers, in case the passenger turned out to be a mugger. The concept seemed unreal to Dianne—people stabbing and shooting other people or hitting them over the head. A chill passed through her. Certainly physical violence would explain Frank's disappearance. For the first time, she realized she might never know what had happened to him. No! Even to know he was dead would be better than never knowing, for the rest of her life, for the rest of the children's lives.

They came to the other side of the park. The West Side.

"Hey," said Dianne, irritably, "I said *through* the park, not *across*."

He pulled to an abrupt halt between Central Park West and Columbus Avenue. "What are you, lady?" he snapped. "An English teacher? Through the park, across the park. Where do you want to go?"

"I wanted to go *through* the park," she answered evenly. "*Now,* I would like to go home."

"Sure, lady, anything you say, lady. Do you have any idea where you live?"

Lips tight, Dianne opened the door, grabbed Jimmy's hand. She fished out a dollar bill and exactly the right amount of change. "Here," she said, shoving it at the driver.

Obviously infuriated by the lack of a tip, he roared away from the curb, too fast. Dianne grabbed Jimmy, pulled him way back onto the sidewalk.

Still angry, Dianne took stock of her surroundings. The whole area seemed a mixture of old and new buildings, ranging from tenement slums to luxury skyscrapers. The streets were not as clean as on the East Side. The stores, here, seemed to shriek DISCOUNT. On the East Side, the word was generally whispered.

"What are we doin' here?" asked Jimmy.

"Looking for a cab," answered Dianne, trying not to sound as irritable as she felt.

To Jimmy, it seemed a logical answer.

Dianne let out a deep breath. She took Jimmy's hand and, unknowingly, started toward Broadway. It had never occurred to her that she might have trouble getting another cab. A passenger would not have to be a mugger, she decided, to mug that driver.

Strange—Dianne was sure she had never been in this neighborhood before, and yet—something vaguely familiar.

Columbus Avenue, Amsterdam, Broadway. At Broadway, she hesitated, then decided to walk—downtown, so that she would at least be headed in the general direction of home. Walk from this subway entrance to the next. If no available cabs appeared in the meantime, take the subway.

At 93rd Street between Broadway and West End Avenue, she saw a large apartment building still under construction. She slowed down. She felt disorientated—as though the lights should be lit, even though it was daylight. Angrily, she forced herself to walk faster. A thought like that was not even sane.

At 91st Street, the feeling was even stronger. Black out the sun, turn on the street, building and car lights. Slowly, purely on impulse, she turned the corner, started back up toward Amsterdam Avenue on 91st Street. A large new apartment building stood on the corner. The feeling was now so disturbing that Dianne tried to find a logical basis for it.

"Frank—" she whispered. Something to do with Frank? Of course it had something to do with Frank—didn't everything, these days?

Jimmy, who had run ahead of her, ran back. "Hey, Mommy, look at the lion!"

"Yes, dear," she answered, not really listening.

"No, it's a *real* one. A bunch of 'em!" He pointed to the building next to the apartment building—an old brownstone with two stone lions flanking an orange door.

Dianne smiled. A "bunch" of them. He could not even count yet. Or, possibly, he had no real desire to. He did seem to know the sequence of numbers up to about ten, but he rarely associated a particular number with a specific quantity of tangible objects.

Dianne disliked the lions. She found their medieval styling too representative of a cruel and violent period in history. Had something cruel and violent happened to Frank? Now standing in front of the brownstone, she looked back at the apartment building.

Frank was—under the ground. Tears flooded her eyes. Under the ground could have only one meaning—dead. Frank was dead. Under the ground. The feeling seemed to come from the earth itself, up through the sidewalk into her body, her mind. Frank is under the ground. Frank is dead!

She ran after Jimmy, now way ahead of her, and her previous feelings seemed to subside, slightly.

Unused to running, out of breath, she slowed down. With deep concern, she realized her feelings at that corner had approached hysteria. At this rate, no doubt she would soon see visions, hear voices.

Jimmy was directly ahead of her. He had fallen into step with a little blond girl beside an elderly woman. Dianne caught up to him and took his hand. Awkwardly, she smiled at the woman. "He's awfully sociable," she said. "I hope he didn't bother you."

Amanda Hilton returned the smile, but conservatively. So many new people had moved into the neighborhood. Occasionally even someone who seemed pleasant at first turned out to be undesirable. However, this woman was nicely dressed— and both she and the child seemed clean. "Not at all," she answered. "He's well behaved."

"At times," answered Dianne.

The light changed.

Amanda and Sarah continued on toward the park. Dianne spotted a cab—three of them, right in a row. She hailed one, then climbed in with Jimmy beside her.

"Where we goin'?" asked Jimmy, already up on his knees for a better view through the window.

"Home," answered Dianne. She gave the driver the address, then added, strictly for her own satisfaction, "Across the park."

The cab radio sent pop music into the back seat and Dianne wished the driver would turn it down—preferably off. The number ended and an announcer's voice came on, high-pressure selling a computer programming course. You, too, can program computers. Oh, certainly I can, she thought dryly. A peculiar sadness touched her—as though she had forgotten or lost something, somewhere back in that neighborhood. Cut loose and run, she thought. Maybe that was what she had lost.

Still—the feeling about Frank had been so strong. *Was* he dead? She searched her feelings, instincts, as Mark had told her to.

No, Frank was *not* dead. Then why had The Word come to her saying he was?

Confused, depressed, she sat back and lit a cigarette. The commercial ended, the local news came on. By this time tomorrow, Dianne would have a private detective on the job. She decided not to wait until tonight—go ahead and disturb Bill at his office. Tonight, she would have to tell the children the truth. She looked at Jimmy, felt the now-familiar tightness of controlled tears.

The news broadcast continued. Airlines trace cause of plane crash to defective radar equipment. City official denies taking bribes.

Just—ask him to turn it off, Diane thought. They weren't all like that other driver.

News bulletin just in. Wildcat Railway Express strike settled.

Dianne's hands were damp with perspiration. Now, she felt

almost as intensely disturbed as she had felt back on that corner. It made no sense, none of it.

Three of the quintuplets born yesterday at New York Hospital are in satisfactory condition.

Dianne leaned forward. "Excuse me," she said. "Would you mind turning off the radio?"

The answer was a sharp click, followed by relative silence.

"Thank you," she said. "I—have a headache."

Without turning, the driver answered, "I got aspirin. Want some?"

Touched, she answered, "No. But thank you."

She leaned back, closed her eyes. Parallel lines, again. She remembered part of the dream. A picket fence. What could a picket fence mean? Somewhere out in the suburbs, the country?

Angrily, she tried to piece it together. Frank was dead—but not dead, somewhere out of the city.

What else had come to her through instinct? Examine feelings. Anything else relative to Frank?

She drew a complete blank.

Perhaps Mark could do better. Abruptly, she wondered, could Mark pick up signals *through* Dianne? If anything beyond the normal range of her five senses had touched her this morning—could Mark pick it up, explain it to her?

She leaned forward. "I changed my mind," she said to the driver. "I'm sorry. Please take me to—"

She gave him Mark Hembric's address.

Chapter Thirteen

"It shouldn't be like this," said Kathy Gillmore. "It's too—unpoetic."

The West Side coffee shop where Mark Hembric sat facing Kathy Gillmore was not quite clean. Warm June sunlight poured in through the unwashed picture window, highlighted each stain, spill and mar wherever it touched the mustard-yellow faded plastic seat covers.

"I mean, a cup of coffee at 11:00 A.M. on a ridiculously sunny, normal Thursday morning," she went on. "Pretty lousy coffee too." She swished the bitter remains around in her cup.

Carefully, Mark answered, "Honey, just relax, okay? You are not Camille. This is not *The Fall of the Roman Empire.*"

"*I hate you!*"

"Is that why you asked me to meet you here? You could have told me that over the phone."

"Mark, I love you," she said. "I love you so much. I—I don't want to live without you. I mean it! You'll be responsible!"

Gently, he answered, "Kathy, do you even know what's real and what's a scene? Now if you want to talk, okay. But plain English. Maybe you do hate me, but don't kid yourself that you love me. And don't kid yourself that you're planning to commit suicide, for crissake."

Avoiding his eyes, she ground out her cigarette in the cheap, chipped ash tray. "You make me feel dirty," she said, more calmly this time. "Like everything we ever did together was cheap and dirty."

"*I* don't think it was either cheap or dirty," he answered, "but your feelings are something you have to work out for yourself."

"I was a good lay, wasn't I?" she asked angrily.

"Damned good, honey. Is that what you want to hear?"

"You said you loved me!" she snapped, close to tears.

"I *do* love you, but I don't want to marry you. I don't want to marry anybody, I don't want to live with anybody. I like my life just as it is. I liked having you part of it."

"Mark, I won't go if you don't want me to." Tears flooding her eyes, she continued, weakly. "You don't have to marry me."

"Kathy, where do you want to be, five or ten years from now? In bed with some other guy talking about how you almost made it as an actress, or do you want to really make it— California—Hollywood?"

She did not answer.

He picked up, fast. "You're one of the most beautiful girls I've ever seen, Kathy, but it doesn't last. Use it—now, so that when it starts to go, you'll have something else—something worth more than what you've got now. A name."

"Would you have loved me if I were ugly?" she asked. The high school dramatics club, again, for crissake.

"How the hell do I know?" he answered irritably. "You're not ugly."

She smiled, but the intensity in those deep green eyes put him on guard. "You'd like to have a name, wouldn't you, Mark?"

Carefully, with forced casualness, he answered, "Sure. Why not?"

"Well, I'm going to help you. There are lots of writers in California. I'm going to find one—work with him on a magazine article about you."

Muscles tense, but still carefully, even though he was reasonably sure what was coming next, Mark answered, "That's nice."

Her smile was syrupy. "I'm going to tell them how you do it, Mark. Everything."

"Well, I don't see how I can stop you. You know, of course, you signed a legal agreement not to. I'll sue you." Abstractedly, he grabbed a paper napkin and toyed with it, angrily. "With that TV series, you'll be worth suing," he continued.

"I hate you!"

"Again? Of course, you might get lucky," he added. "You might not be able to find a publisher."

"Oh, I'll find a publisher."

"Maybe. Maybe not. Have you ever noticed how big, psychic happenings make page one—and the retraction rates a squib on page forty? Magazines run articles to attract readers to look at their advertising. And readers are interested in psychic happenings, not non happenings."

"I'll ruin you," she answered sweetly, without moving her teeth.

He sat back, took his time. Coffee-break workers from nearby shops and offices created a continuing conversational background. "No," he said, "you can't ruin me. People believe in psychic phenomena because they want to, Kathy—even desperately want to. Gives them a sense of power, I guess. Lets them feel they have sources of information other people don't. Maybe it even gives them a sense of immortality. Believe in this, believe in just about anything. Believe it's possible to know and thereby partially control your own probable destiny. You're not going to change that belief, honey. Granted, you might be able to knock a hole in the mind reading bit—*might*. I wouldn't bank on it though. They'd have forgotten the details you're relying on to convince them. And remember —they don't want to believe you. They'd much rather believe me."

"All right. Maybe I couldn't take away the clients you already have, but I could keep you from using that mind reading gimmick to get any more. Once they knew in advance what to look for—"

"That, I'll admit, is possible."

"And I could certainly knock out that parallel lines routine."

"I rarely use that any more," lied Mark.

"I don't believe you," said Kathy. "It's too good. That woman who lost a diamond pendant—you said find the parallel lines. Turned out to be on a window sill under a venetian blind—the slats—the parallel lines."

"By now," answered Mark sharply, "in her mind, I said look on the window sill under the venetian blind."

"Find love by the parallel lines," Kathy went on, contemptuously. "So she meets him between two parallel trees at a summer resort—and that one who met him on a train—the parallel railroad tracks."

"A couple of weeks ago, I got a referral from the one who met him on a train. Kept gushing about how I'd told Gladys she'd meet George on a train."

"It's *obvious*," exploded Kathy, no longer believing it. She glanced around the luncheonette angrily. The menu above the counter, announcing in parallel lines of type the day's offerings. The street, clearly visible through the picture window— the parallel alignment of the sidewalk, curb, street, then curb, then sidewalk. The vertical parallel lines of the buildings, enforced by parallel lines of windows in both directions. Was there anyplace anyone could go where parallel lines did not exist?

"I could also mess up your psychic readings on objects," she persisted.

"Really?"

"Sure. Just tell the owners to keep quiet."

He laughed. "You're dreaming. They can't keep quiet."

"I have a locket," Kathy mimicked. "I see—an injury." Everyone at one time or another in their life suffered at least a minor injury. "A woman—" she continued. Obviously it was a woman's locket. When the owner said it belonged to her mother, Mark knew it was an older woman and—*belonged,* past tense—assumed the mother was dead. And so it continued, with Mark returning whatever information he was fed. Even the most subtle unspoken emotional reaction constituted information, to Mark. On those rare occasions when he fouled up, there were many outs. Interference in the vibrations or perhaps others had handled the object leaving an aura of their lives rather than the life of the owner.

Mark waited, looked at her.

Abruptly, tentatively, she asked, "Mark—do you believe in ESP?"

"I don't know," he answered, honestly. "I don't *think* it exists, but I can't be sure. I know it's never touched my life. Why?"

"Just curious, I suppose. No—more than that. I have a feeling about you. I think you're close to something you want—something big. And when you get it, I think you'll be happy —or as happy as you're able to be."

Startled, Mark tried to keep his face straight. A psychic reading, for crissake—from Kathy.

"You're laughing at me!" snapped Kathy.

"Not me," he answered quickly, but the grin broke through. It seemed to ignite a spark of camaraderie. "All right," she answered, smiling now. Then, quietly, she continued, "I won't tell anyone how you do it, Mark." She laughed. "If you could see your face! Relief, caution. Play it cool, man, don't rock the boat. Is that supposed to be a poker face?"

"I'm sorry if it's inadequate. It's the only face I've got."

Gently, she reached across the table and touched his cheek. "It's a nice face. I love it. Don't be scared. I'm leaving tonight. Plane leaves at eleven forty-five. I'd hoped I could cancel the reservation, but—" she broke off, sat back. Then, "Mark—could I write to you? Maybe call you sometime?"

"Well, sure. I'd like to hear from you."

She smiled, dryly. "Liar. It's okay, though. I'm leaving now. I don't want you to take me home." She rose to her feet. "Good-by, Mark."

Mark, also, stood. "So long, kid. Good luck."

She walked out, quickly—too quickly.

Mark paid the check. He felt irritable, oddly depressed. Empty, yet free. Well, hell, freedom was what he wanted. The rest would pass. Shake it off, wait it out. He glanced at his watch. Eleven-forty. Next client due at eleven forty-five.

He used the luncheonette phone, called his apartment building office and had them connect him with the doorman. "This is Mr. Hembric," he said. "I'm expecting a client in about five minutes, and I'm going to be late. Will you tell her I called and ask her to wait in the lobby, please?"

"I'm sorry, sir. She already left."

"I don't understand. She wasn't even due for another five minutes. Wait a minute—what did she look like?"

"Blonde. About twenty-five. She had a little boy with her."

"Little boy?" Completely at a loss on who the blonde might be, Mark continued, "No, this woman's close to sixty. Gray-blue hair. The blonde—did she say anything, leave a name?"

"No, sir."

"Oh. Okay." Check his answering service and see whether the blonde had left a message, but later. Mrs. Cranston Aldrich, at sixty bucks a session, had a higher priority.

He walked outside, into the bright June sunlight and hailed a cab.

At approximately twelve, noon, Amanda and Sarah Hilton returned from the park. As they entered the inside hallway, Amanda saw a note taped to the door of her apartment. Angrily, she tore it down. Notes pinned on doors were an open invitation to burglars—advertised that you weren't home.

She read it. MRS. HILTON. PLEASE RING MY DOOR-BELL. KATHY GILLMORE.

Irritably, Amanda glanced from the note to Sarah, then back again. Lunch would be late. Seemed that if Miss Gillmore really wanted to see Amanda, the least Miss Gillmore could do was ring Amanda's bell—and keep ringing until she got an answer, the way all of those actresses rang when no one was home upstairs and they had forgotten their keys.

With Sarah in tow, wearily, Amanda climbed the stairs, rang the bell.

"Who is it?" called Kathy. She sounded nasal—as though she had a cold.

Instinctively, Amanda stepped back, with Sarah, to avoid the germs. "Mrs. Hilton," she answered.

When Kathy opened the door, Amanda decided it was a terrible cold—eyes red, voice nasal, nose running.

"I wanted to tell you," said Kathy, "I'm moving out. I'm leaving tonight."

Stunned, Amanda answered, "You can't! Your lease says thirty days' notice."

"You'll get your money," snapped Kathy. "You'll also get another tenant. My roommates already have someone lined up."

Another actress, no doubt. Rage welled inside Amanda. "I'll have to meet her," she snapped.

"I'm sure she'll be thrilled," answered Kathy. She closed the door.

In her kitchen with Sarah, Amanda flipped on the radio. Thanks to that nasty Miss Gillmore, she had missed the twelve o'clock news.

Well, she decided, reaching for the peanut butter jar, it probably did not matter. Those strikes usually lasted for weeks.

"Bug in your milk," hissed Tracy Klaner. "A *spider!*"

"Bug in *your* milk," yelled Jimmy.

"*Stop* it!" exploded Dianne.

Milk—abruptly all over the kitchen table, the floor, the wall—and Tracy. Tracy's milk, the glass still in Jimmy's trembling hand. "Bugs all over you!" he screeched. "Billion, hundred bugs!"

Incredulously, Tracy stared at her saturated dress, wiped some of the drips from her face.

Dianne grabbed the glass from Jimmy's hand. "Go to your room," she said. "Tracy, go take a bath."

"How come you never yell at Jimmy?" demanded Tracy. "You saw what he did!"

"I saw what you did too. You teased him!"

"You don't love me," wailed Tracy, real tears filling her large, blue eyes. "I want my daddy!"

Rigidly, Dianne answered, "Tracy, go take a bath. Jimmy—into your room—by the time I count three. One—two—three!"

Alone, now, Dianne sat on a stool, abstractedly watched the diminishing drip of milk from table to floor.

She called Bill's office.

"I'm sorry," said his secretary. "He's in court today. I expect to hear from him around four. Would you like him to call you?"

Four, Dianne decided, could be awkward, with both children up from their naps. "No," she said. "I'll call him at home later tonight. Thank you." She hung up.

"Mommy, Mommy, I have soap in my eyes!"

Wearily, Dianne walked back to the bathroom.

With Tracy and Jimmy both in for their nap, Dianne decided to make some more phone calls. The police again, then try Mark—home and answering service. At least find out whether he had gotten her message. Also, she had to call the cleaners and, she supposed, the building superintendent to have the kitchen light fixture repaired. She had tried a new bulb—the problem had to be the fixture. Had Frank been home, he could have fixed it. It would have been a lot easier than trying to get action from the landlord. Frank was good with electricity—even fixed her iron, once.

But Frank was not home. She felt unnaturally sleepy. Rejecting the whole mess, no doubt, from the slopped milk in the kitchen to Frank's disappearance.

She cleaned the kitchen then, slowly, walked back to her bedroom. Exhausted, she stretched out on the bed, intending to remain there only a minute or so.

She felt awfully sleepy—almost drugged. Almost as she had felt in the hospital after Jimmy was born when they gave her a pill to make her sleep. Little blue and white capsule.

She closed her eyes. Blue and white? Odd. She now clearly remembered that the capsule they had given her in the hospital was red, not blue and white.

Chapter Fourteen

With hands that trembled, Amanda Hilton emptied the small blue and white capsules into a chipped custard dish. Their contents was a fine, white powder. She tasted it—bitter, like the odor of burning weeds. Strong. Some of the color left her face. She had never tasted the contents before, merely swallowed the closed capsules.

Perhaps—chili. Or maybe she could make some curry.

Ridiculous, she decided. Mr. Klaner would know right away that something was wrong. Of course, Amanda had tasted the pure powder. Anything added to it would dilute it. Perhaps she did not have to rule out peanut butter and jelly—if she used the right jelly, something with a little zing to it.

She now almost wished she had let the lunch dishes remain unwashed, soaking in the sink until dinnertime. Then she would have been out to the kitchen before the one o'clock news came on. But the roaches swarmed over unwashed dishes, occasionally drowning in the dishwater.

The radio was still playing, softly. How long would it take for the pills to work? Amanda tried to remember—half an hour? Well, not really. The effect was gradual, unless they were mixed with liquor. Then it would be only about five or ten minutes, her doctor had warned her. Don't take them after you'd had a drink—they'll knock you unconscious.

She emptied the fourth pill into the custard cup. Four should be sufficient. She only wanted to knock him out. Give it to him now. In an hour or so, before Sarah woke up from her nap, go back down and switch the chains. Tonight, force him to walk to the trunk. First thing tomorrow morning, call Railway Express.

She started to tremble so badly, she had to sit down. Slowly, gently, she laid her hands against her heart and issued a small, frightened prayer that her heart would slow down, continue to beat.

She had already checked with Liz Brown, her neighbor from the apartment building next door. Mrs. Brown would take Sarah in exchange for Amanda taking Mrs. Brown's little girl, on the same basis, at some future date. Amanda planned to be at the railroad station in Burwick when the trunk arrived. She would have it loaded onto a board with wheels inside a drive-it-yourself truck. Her heart pounded even faster. Drive to the lakefront area of her rented cottage, dispose of the trunk, return the rented truck, then catch the next train back to New York.

She closed her eyes, but only for an instant.

Back to work.

Peanut butter and jelly. Best to mix the sleeping pill powder with the jelly. The peanut butter was thicker and would be difficult to stir. Plan ahead. Excellent.

She opened the cupboard door. Jelly. Peach? Strawberry? Grape had a good strong taste. Raspberry would be even better.

She glopped two tablespoons of raspberry jelly into the custard cup, then almost knocked the cup onto the floor. A cockroach! It was all the way into the custard cup. Well, go ahead, she thought. Stuff yourself. You'll go to sleep, then I'll dump you out and step on you.

However, she could not bear to look at it. She took a spoon, lifted the roach out of the custard cup, then dropped the spoon onto the floor. By the time she picked up the spoon, the roach—laden with jelly, was gone.

Feeling queasy, Amanda took a clean spoon, stirred the sleeping powder into the jelly, then prepared the sandwich.

Time seemed to have stopped for Frank Klaner. He felt arrested in some other century, there in the flickering glow of the lantern. What madman had built this place? The old woman could hardly have managed the construction.

The chains which hung on the wall beyond his cell frightened him. He pictured himself trying to explain telecommunications to some sixteenth-century tribunal, then being thrown into a dungeon for heresy.

The lantern light grew perceptibly dimmer. Quickly, Frank rose to his knees, stared at the dying light. It was not the darkness he feared, but rather what the darkness might do to his mind. He had begun to feel human again—coherent and reasonably intelligent. No more sweetly beckoning, then surging, then consuming fantasies. With even the meager light of the lantern, the world and Frank remained real.

The light gave one last flicker, then died.

Frank closed his eyes, realized there were tears in them. Stiffly, he sank down to a sitting position. How much longer, he wondered, did she intend to keep him alive? Did he dare ask her for a pack of cigarettes? Maybe—if he said whatever she wanted him to say, she would bring him cigarettes. Miriam Hilton? If he had not seen the little girl, he might have doubted whether Miriam Hilton ever really existed.

California. He tried to recall every detail of the trip. Ed Lucas and Pete Marshall were with him. Now, if she had accused *Ed*—he broke off.

Ed?

No. His mind was going again. Fantasies. Full-fledged paranoia. Ed wouldn't dare.

Frank lay on his back. If he asked her for cigarettes, what would she say? Across the dimly lit cocktail lounge at the airport, Dianne had mistaken Ed for Frank. It happened constantly around the office with people who didn't know them very well. Offer her the money to pay for the cigarettes. What difference did it make? The money was already hers—everything he had with him. He was hers. Miriam made sketches of Frank—or Ed? But to use Frank's *name?* Granted, Ed Lucas' sense of humor was crude, but—but what? That was it! Ed was half drunk most of the time they were there—probably thought it was funny as hell. Ed and Frank stayed at the same hotel, worked in the same office. If she wanted to check either, yes—Frank was there. Grandma said she met Frank outside his office to tell him she was pregnant—but it was Ed she met, never knowing the difference.

Impotent rage welled inside Frank. Ed Lucas! Break his goddamn neck. Fire him, point blank, refuse him a reference. Fantasies, sweet, so sweet. Fantasies of being free, of physically attacking Ed Lucas. Hey, Ed, I've got a surprise for you. You just trot along home with this sweet little grandmother, and she'll show you something you won't even believe.

Abruptly—light. A small rectangle of light opposite the door to his cell.

Grandma's calling card. Several minutes later, he listened to the grinding squeal of a heavy door, like fingernails scraped across a blackboard. He rose to his feet, weak from inactivity and inadequate food, yet sustained—even strengthened by rage. He felt oddly conscious of the strength in his hands. If he could touch her, he could break her in half, yet helplessly, lifelessly, his hands remained at his sides.

Tell her? The guy's name is Ed Lucas. Take a look at him, you'll believe me. Whatever you do to me, go back and pull the same routine on Ed Lucas.

Amanda drew back when she saw him standing. He had seemed big before, but now he seemed tremendous. In addition, with that matted beard and his clothes now filthy from lying all over the floor—well, he was not anything she would care to meet in a dark alley. Wordlessly, she left the keys against the far wall then shoved the bag containing the sandwich through the bars, away from where he might be able to get his hands on her. She retrieved the now dark lantern and started toward the exit.

"I don't suppose—" called Frank, tentatively.

She stopped, forced herself to look at him again. Motivated by fear rather than anger, she snapped, "What?"

He bit his lip, kept his voice steady, said the word. "Cigarettes."

"What about them?"

"I'd like some."

"No."

She left, carrying the lantern and flashlight with her. The door squeaked, clanged shut.

Yes, he thought, if he could touch her, he could quite easily kill her. He realized he had not told her about Ed. He knew he never would—for his own sake, not Ed's.

There in the blackness, he fished for the lunch bag, then sat down with it, ravenous. Peanut butter and jelly again. He took one fast, large bite then washed it down with Diet Pepsi.

Strange—little bit of an aftertaste. Saccharin? Diet Pepsi contained saccharin, but this was different. Diet Pepsi also contained sugar, and the taste was sweet—pleasant. Okay—what?

The answer seemed obvious. Diet soda—diet jelly, but the jelly contained much more saccharin, no sugar. He finished the sandwich.

Kathy Gillmore, successful in switching her reservation to a five o'clock flight, took one last look at the apartment. Mark had never seen it—their meetings were always at his apartment. No roommate problem that way. Kathy wished either of her roommates were with her now, but Jeanne was off on a modeling job and Alice—her other roommate, was doing a TV commercial. For the first time since Kathy had lived there, so often wishing she could afford her own apartment, this apartment seemed oppressively empty—lonely.

She left her keys on the mahogany sideboard, then hoisted her suitcase and started down the stairs. Get away, fast. Run. Away from this building, this city where she had spent so much time thinking of Mark. Why had she booked the original reservation for eleven forty-five? Had she really hoped Mark might ask her to have dinner with him, take her to the airport? Or had she felt that eleven forty-five would give him plenty of time to call and stop her? Not Mark, she realized now, dryly. She would probably never hear from him again. Mark knew how to quit while he was ahead.

At the bottom of the stairs by the front door, Kathy looked at her name neatly lettered on a piece of cardboard inserted in a slot under the doorbell to the upstairs apartment. Awkwardly, she placed her suitcase on the floor, then removed the cardboard. She slipped it into the pocket of her smart green summer suit. With tears in her eyes, she announced to the peeling walls, faded carpet and chipped ceramic lamp, "Kathy Gillmore doesn't live here any more."

Amanda Hilton felt disconcertingly dehydrated. Perspiration. Nerves. She prepared a cup of tea for herself, then sat at the kitchen table. The tea was too hot to drink.

She glanced at the door which led to the basement. Dead weight. The words kept running through her mind. She had barely been able to budge Mr. Klaner to exchange his chains. At least she had realized in time that his hands would have to be handcuffed in front of him rather than behind. With his hands behind him, he would not be able to crawl through the relatively narrow opening between the wine storage area and the basement storage closet.

Well—it was almost over. A few more hours. She dropped a half-grain saccharin tablet into her tea, abstractedly watched it bubble.

"Grandma—"

She jumped, cried out. "Sarah! I've told you many times not to sneak up on Grandma. Where are your shoes?"

"Dunno. What's for dinner?"

"Dinner?" Amanda glanced at the clock. Renewed tension spread through her body. Six-twenty. She had had no idea it was so late. She answered, "Would you like tuna fish?"

Sarah clapped her hands. "Yes!"

Amanda smiled. "All right, dear. I'll fix it in a few minutes. In the meantime, you run along and play. Grandma wants to finish her tea."

Chapter Fifteen

❖❖*❖*❖*

"Who is it?" responded Mark, his voice filtered and slightly distorted by the apartment intercom system.

"Mrs. Klaner to see you, sir," answered the doorman.

"You mean—she's here?"

"Yes, I'm here," snapped Dianne. At six o'clock, she had recruited a neighborhood teen-ager to baby sit, then caught a cab to Mark's apartment.

"Okay," said Mark. "Come on up."

She stepped into the self-service elevator, pushed the button for eleven. How dare he keep his phone off the hook all day and not return his answering service calls? Take it easy, she told herself with forced calm. You don't really know this man— and you need him.

He was waiting for her when she stepped from the elevator. He stood in the doorway of his apartment, with the door open behind him. He wore dark blue slacks—no jacket, this time. His oxford weave button-down shirt was open at the neck, sleeves rolled up. Scuffed black bedroom slippers had replaced the usual highly shined loafers. Traces of a beard were visible on his face. Five- or six-o'clock shadow.

"I called you," said Dianne, sensing that he was in another of his peculiar moods.

"Yeah. I got your messages." He stepped back, allowed her to enter the apartment, then closed the door behind her.

"Then why didn't you call me?" she insisted, her voice half sharp, half pleading.

"Because I already told you, I can't help you." He walked into the living room, poured himself a drink. He held up the glass. "Care to join me?"

"No."

"No, *thank you,* lady. *I'm* not your husband."

Tears flooded her eyes. "What's that supposed to mean? He left of his own will—because of me? Something I said or did?"

Startled, Mark hesitated, then left the glass on the sideboard and sat on the couch. "Look, Dianne, I'm sorry. I'm in a rotten mood. It's got nothing to do with you. Did you hire a detective?"

"Well, no—" she answered tentatively, seating herself in the chair opposite Mark. "Not yet," she added.

"Then what are you doing here? It's not my baby, honey. I wash my hands of it."

"I came here for help!" she exploded. "Psychic help! Mark—something strange happened today."

"A feeling about Frank. A message, but you don't quite know how to interpret it."

"Yes! Unintentionally, I wound up on the West Side. At 91st Street and Broadway, there's an apartment building—"

He covered his reaction. The building was familiar to him. It was next door to the building where Kathy lived—or would live, until about ten-thirty tonight when she left for the airport. "Wait," he said. "I see—an animal. No—an *image* of an animal."

"The building next door!" said Dianne. "Stone lions! Two of them."

"I know," he answered dryly. "I'm familiar with the area."

A flush of color touched Dianne's cheeks. "Then why did you—pretend it was a psychic revelation?"

"Old habits die hard, okay? Dianne, go home." He rose to his feet, indicated that it was time for her to leave. "I cannot help you," he added.

Dianne also stood, faced him. Quietly, she answered, "I wish I were a man. I think I'd attack you."

He smiled dryly. "I'd much rather have you attack me just as you are."

Completely without thought, nerves raw-edged, impulsively, instinctively, she smashed her hand across his face. Equally on impulse, he drew back, grabbed her wrist.

Motivated now by logical thought, he let go of her. "I apologize," he said. "That crack was out of line. You really love him, don't you?"

"Who?"

"Your husband."

"Yes."

"What are you planning to do now?"

"Find another psychic. As soon as I can," she snapped.

"Dianne—don't. Stick with a private detective."

"I intend to use both."

"Do you think a medium might be able to help you?"

Lips trembling, she answered, "You mean—he's dead and you don't want to tell me?"

"I mean exactly what I said."

"All right. I *hope* a medium couldn't help me."

"If you found a psychic who told you he was dead—what then? A medium?"

"I don't know."

"I think maybe you would—eventually. Dianne, you could spend the rest of your life and far more money than you could ever afford running around to psychics. Get off the merry-go-round, okay? Most of the women I see—they want to know whether their husbands will be as successful as the guy next door, will she get hurt if she has an affair, will she and her husband be accepted by the 'right' social strata. As for the ones with real problems—most of the answers are just reasonably objective common sense. But, Dianne, common sense won't help you. You need a detective. You do not need a psychic—me or anyone else."

"Why, you talk as though there were nothing to it," she answered irritably. "As though ESP didn't even exist."

"It *doesn't,* for crissake!"

Her mouth fell open, stayed that way. Then, quietly, "I don't know why you're saying all these things, Mark. And quite frankly, I no longer care." She started toward the door.

Mark blocked her exit. "What would it take to convince you?"

"Mark, thousands of experiments have proved the existence of ESP."

"Experiments with the odds so slanted in favor of you having it, even a cow placing her hoofs on playing cards could come out looking psychic as hell."

"You told me Frank came back for chili. You read my mind!"

On dangerous ground, now, Mark answered, "I did not read your mind."

"Then how—"

"It was a gimmick. And that's all I'm just about to tell you."

"Will you please get out of my way?"

"Suppose you're right. Suppose ESP does exist. So what? You can't harness it, you can't even interpret it until it's all over. Then you look back and say, here's what that meant. But so what?"

"Why are you saying these things?"

"Because I care about you," he answered, sharply at first. Then—more gently, "You're worse than that crazy sister of yours."

"She'd adore hearing you say that," answered Dianne.

"Oh, come on. I like Nancy. But she is one of the most ardent True Believers I have ever met. Tell her the sun's going to rise tomorrow morning, and when it happens, she thinks she had inside information."

"You told me Frank came back for chili," answered Dianne, evenly.

Mark stepped out of her way, walked back to the couch, sat down. "I also told you, I did not read your mind."

"Excuse me if I'm a little dense," began Dianne, still standing. "You said you cared about me. And before I slapped you, you said something about me attacking you—something that in its own nebulous way, now that I think about it, might conceivably have been an opening for a pass. Is that why you don't want me to find Frank?"

"Cardinal rule," answered Mark dryly, "never sleep with the clients. It's no fun. Have to stay on guard, in character, every minute. Oh, I'd *like* to make an exception in your case, but I seem to have a talent for eventually hurting every woman I touch—and I've already hurt you more than enough. I did this to you. You started out with good, healthy skepticism, and I smashed it. Sit down. I'll tell you how I read your mind."

Curiously, she looked at him. He was probably the most unpredictable man she had ever met.

"I said, sit down," he ordered.

Thoughtlessly, obediently, she moved onto the chair opposite him.

"First," he said, "I want your word—as solid as a seal of confession, that what I'm about to tell you *never* goes any further."

Abstractedly, Dianne wondered whether his background was Catholic and realized she would probably never know. "All right," she said. "You have my word."

"Do you remember what you wrote on the card and the envelope that night?"

"Certainly. I wrote, 'What did Frank come back for?' on the card, and on the envelope, I wrote my initials."

"No. You wrote, 'Frank came back for chili' on the card. You wrote 'Dianne Klaner' on the envelope."

"That's ridiculous," she snapped. "I know what I wrote."

"No. You don't remember. The girl who handed you the materials at the door was my partner. Quietly, individually, she told everyone entering that room to write a *statement*, a *fact* known only to them, then to write their *name,* not initials, on the envelope. Then, if you recall, I spent almost an hour on object readings before I started on the envelopes. You don't really need a time lapse like this, but it helps."

Lips tight, Dianne waited.

"Occasionally someone remembers what they actually wrote," he continued, "but usually they assume the instructions they received were somehow different from what the others received—or they assume they heard incorrectly and made a mistake. Doesn't matter, though. I say, *you want to know*—then give enough information to make it *look* like a question. For anyone who still remembers that *they* wrote a statement, *you want to know* means you want to know the complete statement you wrote. You want to know what Frank

came back for. I know Frank came back for chili because it's
right there in front of me, the last word in your statement."

Disconcerted, now, Dianne tried to remember. "But—you
had trouble getting my name right. You said 'Ann.'"

"Of course I had 'trouble' with names. If I'd gotten them
right, right off the bat, would you—would anyone there have
believed there was anything psychic about it? Like psychically
reading the serial number on a dollar bill—always get one
digit wrong. Get all of them right—obviously, you saw them."

"But—the envelopes weren't even open—"

"Of course they were. I opened every one of them, right
in front of you. All I needed was to have the first one open in
advance. Kathy—my assistant, took care of that. In the trade,
it's known as one-ahead. I held up an envelope—any envelope,
while I read what was open in the box in front of me. After
each reading, I said let's open it and see. At that point, the
one I'd been holding became the next one open in the box—
the next one I read."

"But—the locket—"

"What about it? It was obviously a woman's locket, obviously old. Any obviously very old piece of jewelry 'holds
vibrations of death.' Of course the original owner—and probably at least one subsequent owner is dead. No—wait a sec.
Different locket—"

"This was the one where you knew the woman's mother
had been killed in a car wreck."

"I didn't know anything of the kind—until she told me."

"You mean—set up in advance?"

"No," he answered, unintentionally sounding short-
tempered, "she told me right there—in front of you, in front of
everybody."

"Mark, that is not true. Once—maybe twice, she started to

say something, and both times, you cut her off—told her not to give you any information, and she didn't!"

"Of course she did. Try to remember, Dianne. Remember everything she said—she, and all the others."

"I do remember," snapped Dianne. "And I remember what I wrote about Frank too. I wrote a *question*. What you described may be the way some cheap carnival fake operates, but—"

"Well, what the hell do you think *I* am?"

"But how dare you sit there and try to convince me it would work with an audience as intelligent, educated, sophisticated—"

"Is Nancy sophisticated?" he broke in. "You were probably the most 'sophisticated' person there—and it worked with you."

"When I handed you that pen I bought in the stationery store, you got nothing from it. When I gave you Frank's pen—"

"It was an act, honey. I knew that first pen never belonged to your husband. That's face reading, not mind reading. You couldn't even look at me."

"You said—I wasn't even sure I wanted Frank back—"

"Nancy told me." Quickly, he added, "Not directly—she doesn't *know* she told me—like that woman who brought the locket doesn't know she told me about her mother. But even if Nancy had never mentioned anything about you—everyone has mixed feelings about the person they're married to."

"If what you're telling me now is true," began Dianne, voice scathing because she did not believe it was true, "then will you please explain how you knew, before you even met me, that I'd dreamed of parallel lines?"

He closed his eyes, let out a deep breath. "I use parallel lines all the time—I tell that to everybody."

"How did you know I'd dreamed about them? That's one thing I never told anyone except you. Yet, before you met me, you told Nancy to tell me to find the parallel lines in the dream."

"I *never* said *dream,*" Mark exploded.

Lips tight, Dianne rose to her feet. "I still don't understand," she began quietly, near tears, "why you are doing this. Apparently it really matters to you—to convince me you never did anything genuinely psychic. All right, Mark. Your reasons are your business. Good night."

"Hey—" He jumped up. Then, angrily, helplessly, "Dianne—"

"What?"

"Just remember—I have your word. Don't tell anybody how the carnival fakes operate, okay?"

Too furious to answer, she walked out of his apartment, slammed the door behind her.

It's her problem, Mark told himself irritably, not mine. I tried. If it hadn't been me, she'd have wound up with some other psychic. Her sister would have convinced her. He was no more morally responsible, he decided, than he would be morally responsible if someone, of their own initiative, walked up to him and caught a cold from him.

On the other hand, Mark had to admit someone else might not have been as successful in overcoming her skepticism. Mark, in comparing himself with other psychics and in examining results with his own clients, knew he was good—one of the best, even though he did not yet have a name. *Cheap* carnival fake? No—not cheap. Not Mark.

At eight o'clock, Mark looked up Nancy Meyer's number. Nancy's husband, Mark knew from Nancy, considered Mark an out-and-out phony. Admitting nothing, merely tell Bill that Mark was concerned about Dianne. See whether Bill might be able to calm her down—stop her before she drove herself half nuts running around to other psychics. Dianne had said she intended to hire a private detective—maybe Bill Meyer could expedite the process.

"They're not home," said the baby sitter at the Meyer household. "They went to dinner and the theater. Would you like to leave your name?"

"No," answered Mark. "I'll call back," he added, doubting that he would. The call had been impulsive. Dangerous ground. Nancy talked constantly, to anyone who'd listen. If Nancy, even intuitively, caught on—the whole thing could be sticky.

At eight-ten, he called Dianne. If she was really iron-willed determined to stay on the psychic trail, then "admit" he had lied when he said he was not psychic. Keep her with him. At least he would keep at her to get a detective, tell her to go to a qualified doctor if she were sick, advise her intelligently if she ever had enough money to invest. Faith misused by phony psychics, Mark knew too well, could lead to severe emotional pain, bankruptcy—even death. Too often, the most apparently sincere were the most corrupt, or—in slightly nuts genuine sincerity, the most stupid.

The voice which answered was not Dianne's. "Hullo?"

"Er—is Mrs. Klaner there?"

"No. This is the baby sitter."

A four-letter word came to mind. Reach her tonight. Both of them would sleep more comfortably once it was settled. "Do you know where I might reach her?"

"No. I mean, she didn't say. She came back about seven, then called me about eight to come back and baby sit some more. But this time, she said she wouldn't be anyplace where I could call her."

"Oh. Okay. Thanks." He hung up. Soak in the bathtub, go

to bed. Call her tomorrow morning. Abstractedly, he sat back on the couch, wondered where she had gone.

Abruptly, he sat up. Even if she had gone to a movie, she would have left a number—not merely because of the kids, but in case any word came through on Frank. Where was she, with no given destination, no phone number?

Dianne, Mark decided dryly, would probably have attributed his answer to ESP. To Mark, it was a near automatic process of sharply-honed logic interacting with details, even the smallest detail, always absorbed, catalogued, indefinitely retained through years of strict self-training and discipline. Dianne had gone back to that corner at Broadway and 91st Street. He might be wrong, but the guess was grounded in his sharpest "psychic" assets—observation, retention, logic.

He pictured her standing on 91st Street off Broadway, alone, with inadequate street lighting, an inadequate supply of cops and a profusion of drug addicts and derelict alcoholics. Beautiful, blond Dianne Klaner. Black and Spanish faces, switchblades, dark hallways. Ninety-first Street and Broadway was almost the edge of Harlem, for crissake.

Angrily, quickly, he walked into his bedroom, exchanged the slippers for shiny black loafers. He grabbed his wallet, cigarettes, lighter and keys.

Minutes later, wearing a light sport jacket, he reached the street, hailed a cab.

Chapter Sixteen

Dianne Klaner looked at the apartment building at the corner of Broadway and West 91st Street. The area seemed vastly different at night—threaded to a higher pitch, like a record of street sounds with the volume turned up. More people were visible—or perhaps Dianne was merely more conscious of them because so many of them made her uneasy in the way they looked at her.

"¡Chica! ¿Qué tal?"

She swung around, frightened. Two boys—they might have been teen-agers, their faces too perfect, bronze skin, coal black eyes.

"I—I don't understand Spanish," answered Dianne.

"Oh-h-h, *no comprende.*"

"*Ella comprende,*" answered the second, with dry, grinning cynicism.

They walked on, together, continuing to look back.

Dianne fought tears, tightened her raincoat around her shoulders. She could not stay here.

It was hopeless. She felt nothing—nothing but weariness, despair and fear. Whatever had come to her that morning was gone. Had anything come to her? She tried to recall every detail. A sense of—darkness. Mark had told her that wherever

Frank was, close enough to parallel lines to reach out and touch them, it was dark.

She decided to go back to Broadway, have some coffee—clear her thoughts, then come back. Give it a last try—for tonight. She could return tomorrow night—and the next night, and the next.

She walked to the corner and felt disproportionately irritated because the light was red.

"Dianne—"

She swung around, startled. A man walked quickly toward her, down 91st Street, from Amsterdam Avenue. Mark?

"Mark!" Her anger of earlier that evening momentarily forgotten, she ran to him. Tears flooding her eyes, she grabbed his hands. "Mark, help me!"

"I will," he answered, gently. They stood in front of a brownstone two houses up from where Kathy lived.

In awe, Dianne stared at him. "You knew where I was. *Exactly* where I was. I didn't tell anyone. I didn't write it on any card in an envelope, either," she snapped, abruptly withdrawing her hands.

Mark let out a deep breath, controlled his temper. "Dianne, will you come home, now. Please?"

"Why?"

"Because you're not safe here."

"Mark, let me take you to where I first sensed it this morning. This—I don't know what to call it—communication about Frank."

"If I do—*then* will you go home?"

She looked at him, curiously. "I don't know. Why did you come here?"

"I told you. You're not safe."

"Is this—a feeling you have?"

"Yeah," he answered, unable to control the irony in his tone. "It was a goddamn vision."

Wordlessly, lips tight, Dianne started away from him, toward the corner at Broadway.

He caught up, fell into step beside her. "Mind if I tag along? How about a psychic reading? Let's see. If I'd never met you before, it would probably go something like this—"

"I don't mind at all if you tag along," answered Dianne. "Before you got here, two kids tried to pick me up. Play your cards right, you can even pay for the cab when I do go home."

"Cards? Oh, I bet I could really wow you with my card tricks."

She stopped, looked at him. In spite of her anger, she wanted to smile. "Do you really do card tricks?"

"Sure. Let's buy a deck. Go back to my place or yours—"

"That sounds like a pass again."

"It wasn't. I know when I'm not getting anywhere. I'd just like to see you—and me, out of this neighborhood at this hour. We're within comfortable walking distance of Harlem, you know. I just hate to think of anything as pretty as me ending up with a switchblade in my gut, that's all."

She laughed, stopped in front of the apartment building. "You're incredible. Give me a psychic reading."

"Okay. First time I've ever seen you. I know nothing about you. You are—either married, you've been married or you're engaged. That's because you're old enough and you're attractive. You are—moody. During your life, you have hit many highs and many lows. That fits everyone. At the moment, you are struggling with a disturbing emotional problem. That's not reading your mind, it's reading your face. I'd say there was a man involved. A man with slightly thinning hair. You would probably interpret that man to be your husband. To someone else, the man might be a lover—a father—the problem might be illness, the description might fit the doctor."

Seriously, she answered, "This is approximately where I heard it, felt it, knew it—this morning."

Speaking more to himself than to Dianne, Mark answered, "It's incredible. The will to believe. I've never seen it operate like this before. I've never bucked it before. I've always worked with, not against it."

"Stop it," exploded Dianne, near tears.

"Would you believe the girl I worked with—the one who stood at the door and told everyone coming in to write *statements* on the cards, *full names* on the envelopes?"

Dianne hesitated. "You'd tell her to lie to me."

"No. No tricks. I told you I was familiar with this area. She lives right there—your house with the lions."

Startled, Dianne looked from the apartment building to the brownstone next door.

"She can tell you about psychic readings too," Mark continued. "First thing you notice is approximate age. Tell a teen-age girl there's a boy who really cares—tell a boy the same thing about a girl. Tell an older man a young girl is attracted to him. Even if he can't imagine which girl, he'll still swallow it because he wants to—it's flattering. The will to believe weaves its own magic, Dianne. Even distorts memory. The teen-ager comes back and says, 'remember you told me Joe or Sally liked me?' *I* never said 'Joe or Sally,' but that's how they remember it."

"You talk as though people were idiots," answered Dianne.

"Not at all. You're talking intelligence. I'm talking feeling. The feeling works on the intelligence—wears it down. Feeling is what motivates people to personalize the most general statements you could imagine. Let's stick with age—tell a person over fifty, they've known great sorrow during their lives. Everyone, by the time they hit fifty has had sorrow they've considered great. You can also refer to the death of someone close to them. By then, you can reasonably bank on it that at least one someone they cared about is dead."

"That's terrible."

"Look, this girl I work with has two roommates. I've never seen her apartment, never met either roommate. I'll 'read' one of the roommates for you, okay? Tell you right now what I'm going to say. I know both roommates are actresses—both, therefore, probably have a highly developed sense of the dramatic. So I'll use the great-sorrow bit. I'll tell her there's a man in her life. If she looks unhappy, I'll say he's brought her great unhappiness—and, since no woman wants to believe a lousy love affair is her fault, I'll say he's been a real bast—excuse me, rat. On the other hand, if she looks happy when I first mention him—the rest follows accordingly. I'll even throw in an initial. Pick a letter—any letter."

"Pick a card," echoed Dianne, "any card." Mark, she decided, was possibly slightly insane. But charming. Yet why was he still so determined to convince her he was a fake? Perhaps—if she agreed to see the girl—went along with him, she could discover his motivation. If a key existed by which she could regain his help, she wanted to find it. So many professional psychics *were* fake. At least Dianne knew Mark was real.

"She will attach some great significance to whatever letter you choose. In time, in her memory—unless Kathy tells her how it works," he added dryly, "and I don't think Kathy will, I will have given her not only the initial, but whatever information *she* supplies on whatever name she decides it stands for."

"K," answered Dianne, with forced lightness. Then, all

traces of lightness gone, she continued, "K for Klaner. Frank Klaner."

He hesitated, angry because she was hurt and he was unable to help her. "Couldn't you come up with 'R' or 'J'? They've got a much broader spectrum." Then, quickly, "Okay. You came up with 'K'. We'll stick with 'K'."

They walked to the brownstone with the stone lions, the orange door. There were two doorbells, each with two names posted underneath. The upstairs names were Alice Logram and Jeanne Harris. Downstairs, the names were A. Hilton and Miriam Somethingorother—the letters were unclear.

"What's wrong?" asked Dianne.

"I'm not sure which apartment," he answered. He stepped back—saw a light in the downstairs window, none upstairs.

He went back up to the orange door, reached for the downstairs bell.

With hands that trembled so badly she could barely manage the key, Amanda Hilton unlocked the kitchen door that led to the cellar. She carried with her the poker with which she had hit Mr. Klaner the night he arrived. She flipped the switch that lighted the washing machine area at the other side of the basement. Light from the kitchen poured down over the badly squeaking step, the wrought-iron railing, the gaping steamer trunk on the floor beside the railing. She planned to tell Mr. Klaner she was setting him free—that she now realized he had told the truth when he said he never knew Miriam. The blindfold, she would explain, was to prevent him from telling the police the location of the cage. The chains were to prevent him from harming Amanda because, she would tell him, she realized he was probably quite angry with her. She slipped the key ring into the pocket of the plastic coverall apron she wore over her flower print house dress, then stepped onto the first squeaking step. She felt the board give, slightly, under her weight. As usual, instinctively, she grabbed the wrought-iron railing. This time, however, she found herself staring into the empty trunk. She planned to bring Mr. Klaner to the kitchen doorway, up these stairs, then hit him with the poker and shove him over the railing, into the trunk.

She closed her eyes, turned her face away. What if her heart gave out? How much tension could any human being endure— even a human being younger than Amanda, without a family background of heart trouble?

She flatly refused to review the details of killing him. She would use the poker, quickly, after he was in the trunk. For insurance, she had a knife under the stairs, next to the trunk.

"Please, God," she whispered, "sustain me."

She felt somehow bathed in the light from the kitchen. It was almost as though Miriam were guiding her. Miriam, Amanda's parents, her grandparents—all of them.

Tears flooded her eyes. Her strength would not fail. Its source was divine. Standing straight and tall, even though her knees barely supported her, she continued down the cellar stairs.

A buzz—loud, stark, sharp. She screamed, dropped the poker, grabbed the railing with both hands for support.

The outside doorbell!

No longer able to stand, she sat on the bottom step.

The buzzing continued. She broke into a cold sweat. It was almost nine o'clock. Nobody decent rang doorbells, without having called first, at nine o'clock at night.

For one split second, the sound stopped—then started again. Amanda rocked forward, covered her ears with her hands. Pain raced through her head—started in her ears, spread quickly behind her eyes, into her eyes, up into her temples.

Standing on the front doorstep, Mark Hembric gave Dianne one fast sidelong glance, then—again, leaned against the doorbell. Upstairs bell, also. Maybe Kathy lived upstairs, was trying to catch a nap before leaving for the airport.

Amanda's teeth were actually chattering. She needed a sweater, a blanket.

Then—slowly—yes. The wellspring of God-given strength which she had stumbled onto before returned, flowed through her. She would be all right. A slight lightheadedness remained, also she realized her knees were not completely steady, but she was on her feet, walking. Walk up the cellar stairs, through the kitchen, the hall, the living room.

Numbly, mechanically yet quickly, she removed the plastic apron and tossed it, key ring still in the pocket, into the bathroom. She slammed the door closed. Rage welled inside her. One of those nasty actresses had forgotten her keys, again. How dare she ring like that, never stopping, never caring that Amanda might have been—busy. Amanda flipped out the living room light then peered through the window, but whoever was ringing, ringing that bell was beyond her line of vision. She let the curtain fall back into place and switched on a small table lamp. Now she could see her way to the buzzer which would open the front door. She pushed it, then opened the drawer in the sideboard which contained her spare upstairs keys. The outside bell stopped. The comparative silence was so stark, Amanda wanted to scream. Even though she knew it was one of her upstairs tenants, she half expected some wine-soaked derelict to step in and murder her.

Seconds later, the inside bell rang.

Amanda opened the door—wide. Her mouth fell open, her startled intake of breath almost a scream. She stumbled backward, lost her balance and fell.

Chapter Seventeen

✳✧✳✧✳

"Good Lord!" said Mark. Reacting almost instinctively, he stepped inside, took Amanda's arm and helped her up, onto the couch. "I'm sorry," he said. "We were looking for Kathy Gillmore."

"Can I get you anything?" asked Dianne. "Water?" Vaguely, Dianne recalled having seen the woman before. Yes—that morning, near Amsterdam Avenue.

It was another few seconds before Amanda was able to speak—seconds in which she assured herself that these people had not come to hurt her. Dianne's face was remotely familiar, although Amanda did not consciously remember having seen Dianne before.

"No," answered Amanda, forcing the word. They wanted to run all through the house—find the apron in the bathroom, the open cellar door, the trunk. "No!"

"No *what?*" asked Dianne.

Able to think more clearly now, Amanda answered, "No water. I'm all right, now. Thank you. I was expecting someone else. You see, I rent the upstairs apartment, and I thought you were one of the tenants. I thought one of them had forgotten her keys."

"I rang the upstairs bell," said Mark. "No one answered."

"I guess they're all out. You said you were looking for Miss

Gillmore. She doesn't live here any more. Moved out this afternoon."

Some of the color left Mark's face. "I thought she wasn't leaving until tonight."

"Is she a friend of yours?"

Even if Kathy had not told Mark that Kathy and her landlady did not like each other, he would have picked it up from Amanda's emphasis on the word "friend." "No," he answered. "She owes me money."

"Well, I'm not surprised to hear it," snapped Amanda. "They're all actresses, you know, all three of them. Left late this afternoon."

"Come on, Mark," said Dianne, dryly, but gently. "Let's go."

Go where, he thought. End of the line. Dianne Klaner, True Believer, from this moment on. Desperately, he looked at Amanda. "You sure you're all right?" he said.

Still weak, she nodded.

He smiled, gently. "I'm glad," he said. "You've had enough things in your life to upset you—to upset anyone."

Startled, Amanda answered, "I beg your pardon—"

"Oh, look, it's just—mainly it's your eyes, I suppose."

"What about my eyes?" snapped Amanda, disconcerted and —again, frightened.

"You've known great sorrow in your life," said Mark. "Great pain."

Dianne stifled a groan.

"Sorrow? Pain?" Amanda's voice trembled. Miriam!

"I'm sorry," said Mark. "I've intruded. I had no right to."

"No," said Amanda. "Please—what else?" More frightened now, she wondered who he was. Policeman? Ridiculous.

"I see that you're a sensitive, creative person," Mark continued. Everyone liked to think of themselves as sensitive and creative.

"What else?" said Amanda, near panic, now. "What else do you see?"

"A man," answered Mark, voice solemn.

More color left Amanda's already pale face. It was the reaction Mark had looked for—the key on whether the relationship was good or bad.

"A man who's caused you tremendous unhappiness," he continued. Then, because most people hurt in an emotional relationship with another person believed the other person had lied to them at one time or another, Mark went on, "A man who's lied to you—"

"No," said Amanda, too quickly, "there's no one like that."

"Well, maybe you don't *know* it was a lie," he answered, covering himself, although from the speed of her reaction, he realized she did know. "Someone close to you," he continued. "Or close to someone you feel strongly about." This was to broaden the base for association when he brought in the initial. Quickly, he glanced at Dianne, then turned back to Amanda. "I get the initial—'K'."

K-L-A-N-E-R. Her voice barely more than a whisper, afraid to ask what else he knew, Amanda asked, "How do you know?"

"It's a gift," he answered quietly. "In time, I could tell you a great deal about yourself." He tried to recall the gist of what he had said to Dianne. "You have an aura—a quality—everyone does. I sense it, tune in on it."

"My goodness," said Amanda. "Do you tune out?"

Startled, but covering fast, Mark answered, "What?"

"Well, you're tuned in on me. Will you just forget me, after you leave?"

"Oh, I don't think so."

"You mean you'll go on—knowing things?"

"Mark—" cut in Dianne, her voice dry. "I really do think we should go."

"Go?" snapped Amanda, fighting panic. "But you can't go!"

"We have to," answered Mark, eager now to talk to Dianne alone. "I can see you have something extremely important on your mind. Something pending—incomplete." Obviously she had something she considered important on her mind—she was a nervous wreck. *Pending—incomplete* was standard. Everyone always had something pending. Could be anything from unwashed dishes to a multimillion dollar merger. Strange, though. Amanda was not feeding him information. At least not voluntarily, like most of them did.

Amanda rose to her feet, gripped the arm of the couch to retain support. "Please don't go," she said, fighting panic, "I'm still not well. You frightened me so. My heart—I have trouble, sometimes. The way it beats—"

"Would you like me to call a doctor?" asked Dianne, touched and concerned.

"No! I—give me your name. If I hear from Miss Gillmore, I'll tell her you stopped by."

"I'd just as soon you didn't," answered Mark quickly. "I mean, as I said—she owes me money."

"Don't go," persisted Amanda. "I—let me fix you some tea." The tea she had in mind was heavily spiced.

"No," said Mark. The room was becoming irritating, and so was she.

Gently, Dianne touched Mark's arm, looked at Amanda. "That's kind of you," she said. "We'd love to stay. But you sit and rest. Tell me where the things are—I can make tea."

"I wouldn't think of it," answered Amanda, once again feeling contact with the divine strength. "As a matter of fact," she went on, "I have something far better." Why not? Had she not been saving it for a special occasion? "Some wine," she continued, "bottled almost a hundred years ago for my great grandfather."

"Oh no," said Dianne, "you don't have to—"

"Nonsense," answered Amanda. "I want to."

Almost mechanically, Amanda's legs carried her down the long hallway—had that hallway ever before seemed so long? Do not take the sleeping pills after you've had a drink, her doctor warned her. Even wine, asked Amanda. Any form of alcohol, answered her doctor. Unconscious in five to ten minutes. On her way to the kitchen, trying to appear natural about it, she stopped in the bathroom, closed the door and opened the medicine chest.

As soon as Amanda was out of earshot, voice low, Dianne said, "Mark, how could you! That poor old woman. How could you be so cruel? You made a fool of her—and look how upset she is. The least we could do was let her give us something to drink. She wants to be kind. She's lonely and she's grateful."

"I never made a fool out of you, did I?" asked Mark, settling himself onto the couch.

"It's stuffy in here," said Dianne.

"I asked you a question," said Mark, carefully.

"I'm having trouble breathing." Slowly, abstractedly, she walked to the fireplace. "Frank?" she said.

"Huh?"

Quite simply, she answered, "Frank was in this room."

"Dianne, for crissake, will you get a hold of yourself?"

Tears flooded her eyes. "Mark, am I crazy? Have I cracked up? It's—a little like this morning."

"Frank was never in this room, Dianne—unless he's got mighty peculiar taste in women."

"How do you know?"

"I know."

"How? It's possible. Anything's possible."

Carefully, he answered, "Dianne—what did you think of the 'reading'? Everything we discussed outside, she took personally."

"Oh, stop it," exploded Dianne. "The things you told me were much more detailed, far more personal. What's wrong with you, Mark? Are you crazy? I don't understand you, I don't understand any of it. *Why?"*

"Dianne, I—" He broke off, helplessly.

Trembling, she closed her eyes. "I think I hate you," she said.

Carefully, Mark answered, "Dianne, sit down."

"I feel so close to him," she whispered. "Right now."

He rose to his feet, walked to where she stood. "Okay," he began quietly. Dianne Klaner, True Believer—keep her with Mark. "I did lie to you," he went on. "Remember I told you —a sense of danger?"

In numb confusion, with tear-filled eyes, she looked at him, waited.

"I was afraid for you. Afraid you'd try to go to him."

"If you know where he is," she answered quietly, "please tell me."

"I can't place it in time," said Mark—his constant cover in case Frank were dead. "But I see a street—dark." Frank had disappeared at night—dark, outside—a street. "You said you felt he was out of the city, but this is a New York street." Even if he had left the city, he traveled a New York street to get there. "But," he added, repeating his cover in case Frank *had* left the city, "I can't place it in time."

"Go on," said Dianne.

"A bar," answered Mark. Standard when an adult male was not where he should be. Even if Frank did not drink, it was virtually guaranteed that he had walked past at least one bar.

Dianne waited, listened.

"That is all I am going to tell you," Mark concluded. "Except—I repeat, hire a private detective. I give you my word, I'll work with him—tell him everything I can get. Dianne, a detective can check leads—even psychic leads far more safely and effectively than you can. This is why I lied to you. Some of what you've picked up on your own is valid and dangerous. I thought if I could knock out your faith in ESP, you'd stop trusting yourself, stop acting on your own. You'd also be in no danger of going to another psychic—one who might tell you too much or might turn out to be phony. But the main thing I hoped lost faith in ESP would influence you to do is—Dianne, I *repeat*—hire a private detective."

"I knew there was a reason—" she whispered. "Mark, thank you."

"Dianne, what happens to your kids if your husband *and* you disappear?"

Quietly, she answered, "You're right."

"I'll take you home."

"No. I'll be okay, really. Broadway's just around the corner. It's brightly lit—crowded. I'll get a cab. We can't both walk out on that poor old woman. You stay—please. Apologize for me, drink her wine and be nice to her."

"Let's both wait. We can make it fast."

"Mark, I can't breathe in this room. I feel like I'm ready to start screaming. I've got to get out. And, besides"—she smiled—"if you took me home, we both know I'd keep pumping you. Good night, Mark."

Reluctantly, Mark respected the raw-edged determination in her voice. "Okay," he said. "I'll stay. Good night, Dianne."

Still badly shaken, Amanda Hilton returned to the living room. She carried a plastic tray which held three large filled wine glasses. Her hands trembled, the glasses clinked against each other. Mark took one look at her, then—quickly, took the tray from her hands and set it on the coffee table.

Her face pasty white, Amanda asked, "Where's your friend?"

"Huh? Oh. She didn't feel well, so she left. She asked me to apologize for her." Get it over with, he thought. He reached for one of the wine glasses.

"No!" said Amanda, too fast, too shrilly. "I mean, sit down and let me serve you."

Irritably, Mark sat on the flowered couch. She's nuts, he decided. As inconspicuously as possible, he checked his watch. Nine twenty-eight. Give her approximately ten minutes—because Dianne had asked him to.

Amanda settled herself onto the faded red velvet wing back chair beside the couch. She attempted to hand Mark a glass of wine, but her hands were unsteady.

Mark lifted the one she indicated. The taste was peculiar —not unpleasant. Heavy, sweet yet faintly, subtly bitter.

Her mind divinely clear, now, Amanda realized that the woman leaving made no difference. There would be only the man, now, and it was the man who frightened Amanda. A mugging in a dark hallway. Happened all the time. A dead man. This hallway would be the one outside Amanda's apartment. As far as the police would be concerned, he visited Amanda, then left. Who knew how the drug got into his system? If they even examined him for drugs, which seemed unlikely.

Her hands much steadier now, Amanda lifted her wine glass—the glass Mark had originally reached for. "I'm sorry I took so long," she said. "I couldn't get the cork out, then it broke up inside the bottle and I had to strain what I poured."

"It's good," said Mark, draining the glass. He leaned forward, replaced it on the tray.

"Tell me some more of the things you know," said Amanda, nervously. She had to keep him there and hadn't the faintest idea what to talk about with him.

To hell with it, Mark decided. He started to stand. "Well, I'd like to, Miss—I don't know your name."

Partly through genuine curiosity, primarily to detain him, Amanda asked, "Can you find out? This—thing you have for knowing things about people?"

"Oh. Well—" He sat back again. This was the lower apartment. Two names by the doorbell. A. Hilton and Miriam Somethingorother. Okay, lady, which are you? He leaned his head back, closed his eyes.

How quickly it worked, thought Amanda. Why, it had not been five minutes since he finished the drugged wine—not even two. Frozen by panic, she remained in the chair, tried to force herself to stand.

Abruptly, Mark opened his eyes. Amanda gasped, involuntarily jerked to the side of the chair farthest from Mark.

Curiously, Mark looked at her. "Look, Miss—obviously you're upset. Maybe I'd better just—"

"No," she said, voice weak and strained. "Tell me my name." Covered with perspiration, she waited, almost hoping he would *not* stay. A coward's way out for her, she decided in near self-contempt. Cowardly and potentially disastrous.

Irritably, Mark sat back again. "Okay," he said, voice distant, solemn. The names under the doorbell. "I get an initial," he went on. "But I'm not sure—it's you or someone close to you. Wait—more than an initial. A name. Like—Mary. Mary Lou. No—Maryanne. No—not quite. Wait a sec—Marion. No. *Miriam.*"

He looked at her—waited for the reaction. Quite a reaction. Her face went chalk white. Also—something else. What? Her face—seemed to be moving. Swinging in slow circles. Whole room spinning. Groggy. Fuzzy. Nausea. What the—? Couch, ceiling—tumbling through space.

Blackness.

Chapter Eighteen

Amanda continued to sit in the wing back chair. Mark had fallen to his right, still on the couch, his right arm oddly twisted under his body like a bend-in-any-direction plastic doll. A trickle of saliva escaped from the corner of his open mouth.

Amanda forced herself to look at him. She remained unable to move. Her body was like some distant weight, wired for action by electricity, but the wires seemed short circuited.

She closed her eyes, prayed without words. God had brought her this far, shown her the way, supplied whatever strength she needed. The divine strength was always near. Amanda needed only to touch it, tap its infinite resources.

She felt surrounded by light, warmed and strengthened by its divine glow. She got to her feet, walked to the kitchen, then down the cellar stairs to the knife she had laid out to use, if necessary, on Mr. Klaner.

Carrying the knife, she returned to the bathroom, again donned her plastic apron. She realized she was crying, but decided that as long as her body continued to function, physical quirks like tears were unimportant.

She returned to the living room and noticed the wine glasses. Wash them, wash the tray. Remember everything.

She pushed the coffee table out of the way, then took Mark's left arm and yanked. No, it would not work that way. She lifted both his feet.

Dead weight, dead weight. Echoes of past thoughts, past torments.

She dropped his feet. Fingerprints on his shoes. Some of the divine strength seemed to leave her, then return as she realized the thought had been a warning—worked for, not against her. She removed a faded needlepoint pillowcase from a throw pillow and dusted his shoes. Shiny shoes. Black loafers.

All right. Get a sheet. That was how she had moved Mr. Klaner. Of course, get a sheet! Otherwise bits and pieces of the rug might stick to this man's clothing.

Feeling faintly dizzy, slightly nauseated, Amanda walked to the linen closet in the bathroom, returned to the living room with a sheet. She had originally planned to roll him onto the sheet, as she had done with Mr. Klaner. Now, however, she spread the sheet onto the floor beside the couch, climbed onto the couch and shoved—pushed, with all of her strength against the nightmarishly large dead weight.

It landed on the sheet with a loud, resounding thud.

Covered with sweat, breathing hard, she tied a knot in each end of the sheet, then sat on the floor and pulled the sheet toward her, inch by inch, moving herself farther back every time the sheet moved.

Breathless, she rose to her feet, braced herself against the doorframe of the door which led to the outside hall. Bolt the door to the street, turn out the hall lamp.

She opened the door to the outside hall.

She screamed—slammed it shut. It was—that actress! Not Miss Gillmore, Miss Harris, standing in the hallway as indecent as you please, kissing some man!

Amanda leaned against the door, braced herself against the doorknob, head back, eyes closed, mouth open as though in pain. Dear God, had they seen him, all twisted and pale and drooling, lying there by the doorway with the knotted sheet underneath him?

"Good Lord," said a male voice beyond the door. "What was that?"

"My landlady," answered that nasty Miss Harris. "She's a little off."

"A *little?*"

"You should see my apartment," laughed Miss Harris, that despicable Miss Harris. "She decorated it herself—in spring, with bluebirds in her hair and a rose between her teeth."

Tears flooded Amanda's eyes. They were laughing at her. It was a lovely apartment, it was—her thoughts seemed muddled. She stepped away from the door, almost stumbled over the man in the sheet.

She sat in the wing back chair. They had not seen the man on the floor, Amanda decided. Or, if they had, the sight had not registered. But Amanda had screamed. That, certainly, had registered. When the police found him tomorrow morning and started asking questions, Miss Harris would remember Amanda's scream.

She looked at the man in the sheet. Terror turned to physical pain, centered in the area of her heart, as she continued to look at him. The man was—eerie. He had been unconscious, once, then immediately regained consciousness to give her Miriam's name. He was liable to stand right up, dust himself off and walk out—or kill Amanda. God only knew what that man might do.

Obviously, because she had screamed, Amanda could not leave him for the police to find. There was only one alternative.

The cage.

Gently, lovingly, the divine answers came to her. In the

attic, she had a second trunk. When the Railway Express men came to pick up the first trunk, ask them to move the second trunk from the attic to the basement.

Inward sobbing racked her body. She so wanted to be finished with all of it. Perhaps Liz Brown could keep Sarah for an extra day or so. The two trunks should arrive at the Burwick station within a day or two of each other. Perhaps Amanda could stay at the cottage—take care of both trunks in one trip.

Wearily, in control of herself now, Amanda rose from the chair.

By the time Amanda reached the cage with the unconscious Mark, tied and taped with a pillow under his head, she could barely breathe. Every muscle ached, she longed for sleep. In the glare of her flashlight, she looked at him, now, in front of the cage. Her previous fear of a heart attack seemed to engulf her. She was too old—yes, use the word, too old and frail. Her body, even in its youth, had never been designed to tolerate strain this severe. The strength which had brought Mark this far stemmed from iron will—the willingness even to die, but to pull, push, tug.

A few more feet—into the cage.

Before opening the door, she beamed the flashlight through the bars. "Mr. Klaner," she called weakly.

No response, no change in the pace of his heavy breathing.

Carefully, Amanda unlocked the cage door. "Mr. Klaner, I've decided to set you free."

He groaned, mumbled something incoherent. The chains rattled, briefly, and Amanda drew back. *Could* he walk to the trunk? Perhaps he was still too drugged.

Panic.

No, it was all right. She could take care of it tomorrow

morning. Set her alarm for 5:00 or 6:00 A.M., long before Sarah was awake. Perhaps tomorrow morning would be better. Keep the time lapse until Railway Express picked up the trunk at a minimum.

Wearily, tensely—awkwardly, she removed the adhesive tape from Mark's hands and chained his wrists. She had not originally chained Mr. Klaner's wrists, but Mr. Klaner was not— strange, as this man was strange.

Tears flooding her eyes, she pushed, pulled, tugged, dragged Mark into the cage, then fastened the leg iron, which she had used on Mr. Klaner, around Mark's ankle.

Carefully, quickly, she left the cage, closed and locked the door behind her.

She partially walked, largely crawled back up to the basement. The kitchen door was ahead of her, light pouring down over the stairs. Was this the divine light she sought, she wondered, or merely a perfectly ordinary lightbulb?

She lifted the poker from where it had fallen to the floor and laid it one step below the top step. Hanging onto the railing, she closed the kitchen door—tested. Yes—with that burned-out lightbulb, the cellar stairway area was almost pitch black. Amanda would walk ahead of him, leading the way, then grab the poker. She clung to the railing, now her only guide up the stairs to the kitchen door. She opened the door, blinked at the light, then sat at the table, rested until her breathing became relatively normal. Her arms she discovered with curious surprise were covered with goose flesh. It was that second man. Even chained, he might—what? The prospects were unthinkable, unearthly. She stared at the cellar door, half expecting the knob to turn any second. Slowly —*was* it turning?

Of course not. She whimpered, tried again to make contact

with the divine light. She looked up at the kitchen fixture, then turned away, blinking. A perfectly normal electrical fixture. Again, she rested her eyes on the cellar door, with its shiny brass doorknob. Electrical fixture. Doorknob. Electrify —the doorknob.

The man who repaired the refrigerator had warned her, explained all of it. My goodness, Amanda even had an outlet next to the cellar door—that special outlet for the dishwasher. Take a perfectly ordinary wall plug, plug it into the outlet, then cut the cord, separate the two wires within the cord. With one wire attached to the iron railing by the cellar stairs and the other attached even to the kitchen side of the doorknob, anyone touching the railing and the doorknob at the same time would not only die, with any luck at all they might even fall into the trunk.

Quickly, with the renewed strength of intensified nervous energy, Amanda set to work.

Groggy, sick and in pain, Frank Klaner opened his eyes to the familiar blackness. He reached for his head, discovered his hands were handcuffed. Incredulous, he yanked his wrists the length of the chain, felt the iron bite into his flesh. Full alertness struggled with waves of continued grogginess. He held his breath. Sound—someone else breathing, heavy, low, labored. Mrs. Hilton? In the cage with him? No. She would have heard the rattle of his chains and reacted by now. The breathing would not remain even—unless she were unconscious. If so, Frank's voice would make no difference. "Hey—" he whispered.

No reaction, no change. He started to edge himself in the direction of the sound and realized both his ankles were chained—together.

Obviously, she had drugged him, then come into the cage. Rage welled inside him, directed primarily at what he considered his own stupidity. It must have been the sandwich. He had eaten the goddamn sandwich.

On his knees and elbows, he crawled to the other person. There in the blackness, Frank touched the face—a man's face. Unconscious. Drugged, as Frank had been drugged? But why?

Cigarettes. Feeling vulturous, Frank checked the other man's pockets, still unused to the restricting chain between his wrists. He came up with almost a full pack, plus a lighter. Raising both hands to his lips, Frank took one of the cigarettes, struck the lighter. In its glow, he saw the other man's face, pale and waxen. Tears of impotent frustration formed in Frank's eyes. Help him? Frank could not even help himself. He touched the flame to the cigarette, took a deep drag.

His stomach seemed to heave itself inside out. He gagged, retched, his whole equilibrium seemed to have gone haywire, his mind blank, light-headed, spinning, plummeting, crashing oblivion. Unconscious, he lay on the concrete floor, the cigarette forming a slow ash beside him.

Queasy, dizzy and weak, Frank awakened to the sound of a groan, the clinking of chains. He remembered now. The other man.

"Hey—" said Frank.

Abrupt, unnatural silence followed.

"Relax," continued Frank, dryly. "We're on the same team."

"Who are you?"

"My name's Frank Klaner. Who are you?"

No answer.

"Hey—" said Frank, grateful for the sound of another voice —any voice except Amanda's. "You okay?"

"Yeah, I'm okay. Still groggy, I guess. Name's Mark Hembric. Did you say your name was Frank Klaner?"

"Yeah. Why?" Not daring to hope, Frank added, "Mean anything to you? I mean, are you a cop?"

"No. I'm not a cop. I'm—" Fully alert, now, Mark continued, "A friend of Nancy Meyer. I've been trying to help your wife find you."

"Dianne," answered Frank, his voice unsteady. "Have you seen her? How is she?"

"She's fine—worried sick about you."

"Look," began Frank, almost desperately, "does anybody know you came into this house?"

"Dianne knows."

"Then she'll call the police. But—what did you say your name is?"

"Mark Hembric."

"The police won't be able to find us," Frank continued. "How did you know I was here?"

"A lot of things you'd probably laugh at," answered Mark, carefully.

"What's that supposed to mean?"

"Things like—dreams, instincts, feelings. Mental pictures, occasionally—flashes. In short, ESP."

Frank laughed. "You're joking."

"Yeah," said Mark, "I'm joking. Let's see if we can get out of here."

Gently, Frank answered, "That was my first reaction. Go ahead. Nobody could have convinced me—at first."

"Have you got a shoelace?"

"Huh?"

"Shoelace," repeated Mark. "I'm wearing loafers—no laces."

"Sure," answered Frank. "Got two of them, as a matter of

fact. Won't do to hang yourself, though. Not long enough."
He rattled the chain attached to his ankles. Curiously, he
added, "Why? What are you doing?"

Mark followed the sound, found Frank's foot, removed the
shoelace. "She took my lighter," said Mark.

"Oh. Well, no." Frank groped for the lighter, sat up, felt
more dizzy, more queasy. "Here," he said. "I helped myself
to a cigarette."

"Okay," said Mark. "Let's get some light."

In the glow of the abrupt small flame, Mark saw Frank for
the first time. "Good Lord," he whispered. "Glad I didn't see
you when I first woke up. I—" He broke off, stared at the bars.

Frank misinterpreted. "I told you, we can't get out."

Of all the coincidences which had ever worked in Mark's
favor, this one—was uncanny. Like Dianne coming to this
particular corner. She even said Frank had been in that
woman's living room.

Okay. Maybe ESP did exist.

Maybe.

Mark turned his attention to the handcuffs.

"What are you doing?" asked Frank.

Awkwardly removing his belt, Mark answered, "Keep the
light steady, okay? I'm making a slipknot with the shoelace.
There's a threaded rod attached to a spring inside the handcuff lock shaft. The key screws onto the rod, then you pull
the key. This pulls back the spring that keeps the handcuff
closed—opens it. What I'm trying to do—with the metal catch
on the belt buckle—is jam the slipknot down to the rod. If it
catches the rod—pull. Opens the handcuff."

Numbly, Frank stared at him. "Will it work?"

"Should. May take a while."

"I don't get it," said Frank. "How do you know all this? Who are you?"

"I told you," answered Mark, still working on the lock, "I'm a professional psychic."

"Come off it," snapped Frank. "You also told me you were kidding."

Mark grinned, held his arms wide apart, the handcuffs now dangling from his left wrist.

Frank scrambled to his knees, set the lighter on the floor and held out his handcuffed hands to Mark, fists clenched.

Chapter Nineteen

*

Five-thirty Thursday morning. The alarm clock on the carved mahogany table beside Amanda's canopied bed clanged loudly. Amanda, her eyes red and swollen almost shut from too many tears and not enough sleep, reached out and shoved down on the button, stopped the clanging, felt the sharp cold of the metal against her hand. In semi-conscious terror, she yanked her hand away, as though touched by an electric shock. Electrified metal—electrified metal doorknob. Touch the basement staircase railing and kitchen door doorknob at the same time. Death. Amanda's death. No, this was not the doorknob, it was her alarm clock. Lips trembling, thoughts fading, Amanda pulled the sheet and one faded slightly moth eaten blanket up to her chin, then rolled over and went back to sleep.

Completely free of their restraints, Mark and Frank stood in the flickering shadows of Mark's lighter and looked at the barred door of the cage. Mark indicated the handcuff he held in his hand. "Too small," he said.

"What are you trying to do?" asked Frank, still holding the lighter next to the keyhole.

"The handcuffs—open, they each form a letter 'C'. I was trying to hook that C into the keyhole—twist it, break off the wards." Sensing Frank's confusion, he explained, "Wards are small pieces of metal that let the right key turn—refuse the wrong key. With those out of the way, I could catch the bolt. Wait a sec—that leg-iron hook might be large enough."

"It won't reach the keyhole," answered Frank. "The chain's not long enough. You can't move it—it's imbedded into the wall."

"I can try—" said Mark.

About a minute later, Mark held the leg-iron cuff and swung the attached chain like a jump rope. Clank, squeak, crash—timeworn and rusted, the ring holding the chain to the wall bent to the weight and pressure—twisted, opened. The chain was no longer attached to the wall.

Mark carried the C-hook cuff to the cage door, inserted it into the keyhole. Frank's hands trembled, the light flickered. Carefully, breathing softly, Mark fished with the hook inside the keyhole. Tiny pieces of metal snapped, broke—fell, within the keyhole. The scrape-clank of metal against metal continued. Softly, lips tight, "Got it," said Mark. The bolt slid back, the door opened.

Seconds later, in the dim glow of Mark's lighter, Frank saw for the first time the iron door which had made such a racket everytime Mrs. Hilton came to visit him.

Abruptly, Mark laughed. "This is incredible," he said. "Be careful. She's probably got a rabid alligator out there."

"I doubt it, but take it easy anyway. She's nuts, you know."

"Yeah, I figured that out."

"There's no keyhole," said Frank, his voice raw-edged. "But she used a key—I heard it."

"Maybe the lock's only on the other side."

Frank swore. "What do we do? Sit and wait for her to come back?"

"No. We can take the door off. Lift the pins out of the hinges." He let out a deep breath and removed his jacket.

Approximately fifty-six minutes later, Mark and Frank stood in the cellar, the light from the open storage closet behind them forming an arc in the surrounding darkness.

"There must be a light switch somewhere," said Mark, his voice almost a whisper.

"Looks like a workbench over there," answered Frank. "Maybe—a lamp. Or flashlight."

Lighter in hand, Mark walked to the table. The lighter went out. He flicked it four times, then gave up—pocketed it. He touched the table, ran his hands across the top. Abruptly, he let out a yell, yanked his right hand away and touched it to his mouth, tasted blood. Inwardly cursing, he held his breath.

In a whisper, Frank called. "What happened?"

"Glass—I think. I stumbled over something, grabbed for balance and cut my hand. I'm okay. Hey—flashlight. Let's see if it works." Holding it awkwardly in his left hand, he beamed it at Frank then turned it away, quickly, as Frank instinctively threw his arms over his eyes.

"Sorry," said Mark.

Frank walked to his side. "Wait a sec—" said Frank. "Shine it over there again." Mouth dry, he continued, "Yeah—staircase."

Wordlessly, they walked to it. The staircase consisted of four steps. Mark took two steps up, shined the light on the lock.

Frank waited. Then, "What's wrong?"

Slowly, Mark turned, sat on the second step down from the top. "Forget it," he said, jerking his thumb over his shoulder. "That lock is a solid bronze pin-tumbler."

"So?"

"So you can't open it. Not unless you've got about six weeks and a good saw."

Tight-lipped, Frank answered, "Any windows down here?"

"The ones I saw with the flashlight weren't big enough to crawl through," said Mark.

Frank also sat on the stairs, one step below Mark. In the beam of Mark's flashlight, he noticed an object on the step beside him, and picked it up. A poker—gaudy, ornate—vaguely, unpleasantly familiar. The association registered—was this the poker she had clubbed him with? Instinctively, his hand sprang open. The poker clattered off the edge of the staircase. Mark jumped to his feet, beamed the flashlight toward the sound. Both watched as it clanged into an open steamer trunk lined with faded wallpaper.

"For crissake, take it easy!" whispered Mark.

Numbly, Frank answered, "Sorry."

Mark hesitated, then consciously eased some of the tension from his hands and shoulders. "Okay." Angrily, the flashlight at his side, now, Mark glanced back at the lock. "Hey, it's not locked," he said.

Frank stared at him.

"Look—light from the other side of the door comes through in an unbroken line. I didn't see it before because I had the flashlight on it. The bolt isn't engaged." Awkwardly, painfully conscious of his cut right hand, Mark handed the flashlight to Frank, reached for his wallet and flinched.

"What's wrong?" asked Frank. "What do you want?"

"The lock by the doorknob is locked—it's a catch lock. I need a credit card. One that's laminated. Have you got Diner's Club?"

"I got 'em all," answered Frank, dryly. He braced the flashlight under his arm, extracted his wallet and removed his Diner's Club card.

"Thanks," said Mark.

Standing slightly behind Mark, Frank leaned against the railing, beamed the flashlight onto the lock beside the door-knob.

"No good," said Mark. "Let me hold the light." He took it, braced it under his left arm, then wedged the credit card between the door and the doorframe by the lock. Frank walked to the bottom of the stairs and sat down.

"Okay!" said Mark. His hand on the doorknob, he pushed open the door, stepped up, placed his full weight on the top step. The step squeaked, felt ready to give. Instinctively, he moved backward, lost his balance, the flashlight fell. He let go of the doorknob, grabbed the iron railing with both hands. Frank, behind him, grabbed his shoulders. "You okay?"

"Yeah," said Mark. He yanked his cut hand away from the railing. Rust, grit and flecks of black paint mingled with the sweat and blood of his cut hand. Did he need a tetanus shot, he wondered, or was a shot necessary only if the rusted object was outdoors.

Carefully avoiding further contact with the railing, Mark made his way back up to the door. Funny—the door seemed stuck. He pushed. Abruptly, it opened completely, slammed into the rubber-tipped doorstop.

Mark walked into the kitchen. Frank followed, holding onto the railing. The door was wide open.

Frank stood in the kitchen, felt tears sting his eyes. Sunlight. Six-twenty A.M., according to the clock on that ludicrous pinkish orange wall. Sunlight washed in onto the ceramic rooster on the window sill, the hand-painted flowers, the cracked and yellowed floor. Something on the floor caught his eye—a piece of wire. He followed the line of it, saw it was attached to a plug connected to an outlet beside the door. Irritably, almost instinctively, Frank unplugged it, tossed it onto the sink drainboard. "She's got a little kid here," he whispered. "What's she trying to do, leaving a piece of raw wire plugged in like that—kill the kid?"

Mark held his finger to his lips, indicated silence. "Come on," he whispered. "Let's get the hell out of here."

Quickly, quietly and carefully, they walked the length of the hall into the living room, let themselves out by the front door.

They walked to Broadway. "Dianne," said Frank. "I want to call her."

"Luncheonette across the street," answered Mark. It was the luncheonette where he had last seen Kathy. It had one phone booth.

"I'd appreciate it if you could keep it reasonably short," said Mark. "I'd also like to make a couple of calls."

Frank nodded, stepped into the booth while Mark walked to the counter. He ordered two cups of coffee, waited impatiently.

Ten minutes later, Mark returned to the booth. Frank shoved the door open, looked at Mark with a curious mixture of awe and skepticism. "She said you told her I was in a place that was dark, with bars close enough for me to touch. She said you came to that corner last night, when she hadn't told anybody where she was going, and you told her to go home— told her she was close to me, and it was dangerous."

Solemnly, carefully, Mark answered, "Look, back at the house when I told you how I found you, you said I was kidding —and I said yes. Let's leave it like that, okay? I have a quiet, dignified client practice—people like your wife who need help.

There'll probably be a lot of publicity on this, and I don't want any part of it."

Confused, Frank answered, "But you are part of it."

"Okay—but quietly. I'm not a magician, there's nothing unearthly about it. I'm just sometimes able to—know things, see things other people can't."

"Well, is it okay if I say that much?"

"Well—all right. Okay. The phone—do you mind?"

Frank stepped aside, his instinctive skepticism still lingering. "Dianne's calling the police," he said.

Mark nodded. "Coffee over there is yours." Mark closed the phone booth door, waited until Frank was out of earshot. He dropped in his dime, waited, then dialed information. "Good morning," he said, consciously maintaining an appropriate level of dignity in spite of the grin which continually threatened to break through, "Would you please give me the number of the New York *Times.*"

Dianne Klaner, her eyes filled with tears, looked at the kitchen clock, then abstractedly tightened the belt on her white terry-cloth bathrobe. A quarter to eight. She had called the police at approximately six-thirty, and been informed that Frank would probably be home "in an hour or so." The kids were with her friend Margie who'd promptly agreed to take care of them for the day so Dianne could be with Frank. He would probably be hungry—she wanted to fix him a breakfast he'd love. He so rarely had time for breakfast. When they were first married, he'd liked waffles with maple syrup and sausage. The tears started anew and she wanted to laugh. To cry because the waffle iron had been thrown out years ago and there was no place she could buy a new one at eight o'clock in the morning was ludicrous. She knew the apartment was never quite clean enough to really suit him, although he tried not to complain. She scrubbed the last traces of gook from the splatter shield above the stove, then—disorientated, remembered she had already dusted that hall table he occasionally grumbled about—the table where he had left the yellow tea roses the last night she saw him.

She again turned her attention to making herself look attractive, but it was a lost cause. Tears kept washing away the eye make-up. Finally, defeatedly, she washed her face.

A key—Frank's key. She knew the sound of it, almost by instinct. She ran to the foyer.

He opened the door, walked inside—looked at her.

"Frank—" she whispered, touched and frightened by his appearance. She ran to him, threw her arms around him, repeated his name, softly, over and over. "Frank," she said, "I feel so—helpless. I want to—move mountains for you, cook for you, do something for you, anything, everything. What can I do for you, tell me—what do you want?"

"No," he said, his voice barely more than a whisper, "nothing. You. Just you."